THE
GENERAL'S
HORSEWOMAN

THE GENERAL'S HORSEWOMAN

Carol DeGrange

THE GENERAL'S HORSEWOMAN

iUniverse books may be ordered through booksellers or by contacting:

iUniverse
1663 Liberty Drive
Bloomington, IN 47403
www.iuniverse.com
1-800-Authors (1-800-288-4677)

ISBN: 978-1-4917-4941-8 (sc)
ISBN: 978-1-4917-4942-5 (e)

Library of Congress Control Number: 2014917828

Printed in the United States of America.

iUniverse rev. date: 12/29/2014

Dedicated to my three graces
Roxanne, Deborah and Yvette

CHARACTERS

Wu San Gui (Woo San Gway) --- (1612 - 1678) --- a prominent Ming Dynasty general who joined the Manchu army and helped establish the Qing Dynasty in China --- He was considered by many Chinese to have been a double traitor.

Wu Xiang (Woo Hsi ang) --- Wu San Gui's father who was also a Ming general

Long Qiong (Lung Chee ong) --- Wu San Gui's retainer appointed by Dorgon to ensure Wu's loyalty to the Manchus

Xi Chu (Hsi Chew) --- Wu San Gui's Uighur lieutenant from the far west of China --- Wu's father, the General Wu Xiang, and a Uighur woman were his parents. Thus Xi Chu and Wu San Gui were half-brothers.

Bourtai (Bore tie) --- (1628 - 1686) --- a Manchu princess and great-niece of Nurhachi, who is given by Dorgon as a bribe to Wu San Gui

Mamu --- Bourtai's grandmother and the younger sister of Nurhachi

Girten --- the family servant --- She is treated as part of the family.

Master Yang (Yahng) --- a Buddhist monk who educated Bourtai and her son

Feng Xianfu (Fung Hsian foo) --- a eunuch who had been captured by Li Zicheng's army --- He later became the servant/friend of Bourtai.

Mei Hua --- (1645 - 16??) --- the daughter of Bourtai who was most probably the result of Bourtai's rape by Ma Xun and his soldiers

Wu Gaoxing (Wu Gao hsing) --- Bourtai's son by Wu San Gui

Nurhachi (Nur ha chee) --- (1559 - 1627) --- the Jurchen khan who unified the northeastern tribes beyond the Great Wall of China --- A khan was a chieftain of a clan or tribe. Nurhachi became the Grand Khan of the Manchus.

Abahai (Ah ba high) --- (1592 - 1643) --- Nurhachi's son who declared himself emperor and ruler of the northeast --- In 1636 he founded the Manchu Qing Dynasty.

Fulin (Foo lin) --- (reigned 1644 – 1661) --- the first Qing emperor of China who ruled as the Shun Chih Emperor with Dorgon as his regent

Dorgon (Door gone) --- (1612 - 1650) --- a Manchu prince, the younger brother of Nurhachi, and the regent for the Shun Chih Emperor Fulin --- He was the uncle of Abahai and great uncle of the Shun Chih Emperor.

Li Zicheng (Lee Zi chung) --- a former postal clerk turned bandit who organized a peasant army and overthrew the last Ming emperor --- He had little influence over his soldiers as they raped and plundered Peking. Thus, he failed to establish himself as emperor during the short time he was in the capital before Wu San Gui and the Manchus arrived with their troops.

Jing Yu --- Wu San Gui's wife

Chen Yuan Yuan (You ann) --- the celebrated beauty who was Wu's principal concubine

The Kangxi (Kong hsi) Emperor --- (reigned 1662-1722) --- He attained the Qing throne at the age of 15. Because of Wu's part in the Rebellion of the Three Feudatories in 1673, he became the enemy of Wu. The Kangxi Emperor ruled wisely with intelligence, order and severity.

Ma Xun (Ma Hsun) --- Li Zicheng's lieutenant who tortured Bourtai

Wu Xiang, Wu San Gui, the Kangxi Emperor, Nurhachi, Abahai, Li Zicheng, Fulin (the first Qing emperor of mainland China), Dorgon and Chen Yuan Yuan were historical figures. I have tried to stay true to the facts of their lives.

Bourtai is a fictional protagonist. All of the people in Bourtai's family are also fictional characters. Ma Xun, a minor character in the story, is also fictional.

Chinese surnames are given first, followed by a person's given name.

A GENERAL OVERVIEW OF THE HISTORICAL BACKGROUND

Toward the end of the Ming Dynasty in 1644, the imperial court had become extremely corrupt. The emperor was ineffectual, and the tax burden upon the Chinese citizens was unsustainable. Rebellions aimed at the capital, Peking, had arisen in both the northwest and the south. The southern rebellion, under the leadership of Li Zicheng, was the most capable and the most threatening.

In the spring of 1644, the Ming General, Wu San Gui, was ensconced with his army at Shan Hai Guan, the easternmost fortification of the Great Wall which ended at the Bo Hai Gulf. The Ming Emperor sent General Wu there with his army to protect China from an invasion of the Manchus in the northeast.

The Manchus were a powerful federation of tribes, clans and ethnic peoples which stretched as far west as Eastern Mongolia. Nurhachi, a great shaman and king, formed this confederation using various means such as negotiation, warfare, and subjugation. In 1616, Nurhachi pronounced himself Grand Kahn of the area and named his subjects Manchus. In May of 1621, he moved his capital to Mukden (present-day Shenyang) and built a palace there in the manner of the Forbidden City in Peking. He organized a Banner System of troops under units of Mongols, Russians, Koreans, Manchus and others. These bannermen comprised a powerful fighting force.

Much historical controversy exists as to what prompted the Chinese General Wu to ally himself with the Manchus. As a general, he was most of all a pragmatist and must have realized that even his large army was not strong enough to return to Peking and restore the existing Ming Dynasty alone.

In addition, conflicting accounts exist as to what actually occurred in communication between Wu and Peking and Wu and the Manchus. Some historians have suggested that he made the first overtures to the Manchus suggesting collaboration. It is difficult to guess what Wu had in his mind at the time. We do know about the pressures on him once Peking fell to Li Zicheng on April 25, 1644. The rebels captured, tortured and killed Wu's father who was also a Ming general. Li also gave Wu's favorite concubine, Chen Yuan Yuan, to one of his generals. Somehow Wu learned about these events.

It is hard to believe that Wu was naïve enough to expect that once his army along with the Manchu army had captured Peking, the Manchus would not take a large bite of the spoils. Wu, himself, may not have known what could happen; however, it remains the case that he was a pivotal force in the history of China in changing the imperial rule from the *han* Chinese to that of the Manchus who then established the Qing Dynasty that continued until 1911.

Author's Notes

As an historical figure, General Wu San Gui had much influence in the establishment and subsequent development of the Qing Dynasty from 1644 on. I have tried to adhere to the facts of his life and the actual events in which he was involved.

Scholars have documented Chinese emperors well, especially the Kangxi Emperor. However, because many historians of China consider Wu a traitor and eventually a double traitor, not as much is known about the details of his life other than his role in relation to the governments of the times. The fall of the Ming Dynasty and the eventual establishment of the Qing Dynasty and Wu's part in it is fact. The peasant army of Li Zhicheng and the opposing maneuvers of the Manchu army under the power of Dorgon combined with Wu San Gui's army are also historical events.

The protagonist, Bourtai, is a fictional character. The practice of Chinese men of power was to have a number of concubines, possibly several wives, and in the case of military men, short attachments to other women at various postings.

I have chosen to make Bourtai a fictional, but constant, if sometimes distant, presence in Wu's life. I hope her actions and her appraisals give the reader some perspective on the character of this complex man and his place in Chinese history.

The Romanization of Chinese and Manchu names is different according to which system historians are following. For instance, Wu San Gui is also referred to as Wu San Kuei or Wu Sangui depending on the historian who is writing about him. I have chosen the modern *pinyin* spelling of places and characters and have tried to be consistent. But, I have kept the old spelling of Peking rather than Beijing and the old Romanization of Canton rather than its present designation as Guangzhou.

Places and Terms

Mukden --- the capital of the early Qing Empire which was established by Abahai --- It eventually became Shenyang (Shen yahng). The palace of those first rulers is still open today for visitors.

Goo Gong (The Forbidden City) --- the huge city/palace compound in Peking (Beijing) which housed the Emperor of China and his many wives, concubines, and eunuchs

Yunnan (You nan) --- a wild province in southwestern China which was given to Wu San Gui along with the province of Guizhou (Gway joe) by the Qing Emperor as a personal fiefdom to reward Wu's services to the new Qing Empire --- Wu later came to control much of what is now known as Sichuan, Shaanxi (Shan hsi), and Guangxi (Guong hsi).

The Banner System --- the organization of the Manchu army into units of Mongols, Russians, Koreans, Manchus, and other non-Manchu soldiers under various colored banners which gave each group a sense of unity

The Three Feudatories --- areas in the south of China that the emperor gave as separate fiefdoms to the Chinese generals who had helped the Manchus overthrow the Ming Dynasty. The generals were:
Wu San Gui --- prince of Yunnan and Guizhou
Shang Kexi --- prince of the feudatory in Guangdong Province and surroundings
Geng Jingzhong --- prince of the feudatory in Fujian Province and surroundings

Eunuch --- a man whose sexual organs were removed in order to make him suitable to work in the palace of the emperor among the various courtesans --- Many eunuchs gained great political power.

Memorial --- a message to the emperor that went directly to him --- His cabinet members did not see the memorial.

Xiao --- a term of endearment meaning little child

Putonghua --- common Chinese language

CHAPTER 1
1644

The advance scout came galloping into camp. He reined in his horse, jumped from the saddle and ran shouting towards the general's tent. "General! General!"

Wu came out of the tent. He looked at the scout and said, "Calm down, calm down. What is your news?"

The scout, still breathless, cried out, "Li Zicheng and his army have advanced so rapidly from Peking that they are close enough to engage us in battle by morning."

Wu thought for a moment. Then he gathered his counselors and lieutenants in front of the tent. "We must be ready for battle at sunrise. Our soldiers are to rise two hours before dawn. That gives them time to prepare their weapons. I will have the cooks distribute rice cakes and tea to everyone at that time. We are prepared, but I need to alert my men. I want our most reliable scouts to be in front of our first flank. Fortunately tonight's full moon will make it easy to detect any advances from Li's camp."

I was excited by the idea of the coming battle. The previous night I asked to be able to watch the battle from the hill to the north. Wu agreed, but told me that I must be accompanied by several of his men as guards.

Early the next morning, I stood on the hill. Below me, the soldiers' armor shone splendidly in the sun. I strained my eyes to see Wu who was at the front of his troops, arrows on his shoulder and his sword in his hand. His hair whipped in the wind.

He rode out eagerly toward Li Zicheng's men. He instructed his own men to attach white pieces of cloth to the backs of their armor so that they could be distinguished from Li's rebels when the Manchus joined Wu's army. Wu's men were in the vanguard where they took repeated casualties—casualties so severe that Li seemed about to defeat them. But around noon, a horrible dust storm arose over the field obscuring everything. I lost sight of Wu and prayed that he was all right. It was impossible to see anything because of the dust. The battle raged fiercely in a confusion of men and horses. I could see men crawling away from the center of the storm. Many were screaming. Some were missing an arm or a leg. Others had arrows sticking in their bodies. The cries of the men and horses mixed in an awful din which sounded as though the world was ending. I tried to see through the dust, but the whole scene seemed like ghost armies inside a whorl of sand and earth. Wu's army made repeated charges but was driven back and had many casualties inflicted on it. However, before Li's men could claim victory, under the cover of the blinding dust cloud, the Manchu army appeared in a great clatter of horses and men. They pulled around Wu's right wing and attacked Li's left flank. Li's men turned suddenly to see an army of formidable warriors with shaved heads bearing down upon them. Li's retreat turned into a confused rout.

On that one day, I saw enough of battle for a lifetime. I expected the battle to be heroic, but instead, it was a slaughter.

The stragglers from Li's army were cut down, but I learned later that many made it back to Peking where they vented their frustration by burning many buildings in the city and completely destroying residences of the wealthy after looting them.

Unnoticed, because of the flying dust, several of Li's men strayed northward to the hill where I was standing. Suddenly, a number of riders came straight toward us. One of my guards cried out, "It is Li's men. They must have skirted to the north of our campsite last night."

The guards pushed me and my horse behind a large boulder. The next thing I heard was a slapping twang. The soldier nearest to me slid down the side of his horse. Another looked down with disbelief at an arrow protruding through his back and out his chest. The last two of Wu's men turned to fight, but they were greatly outnumbered and were killed immediately. I heard their cries. Then Li's men scurried around the boulder where I hid. Before I could turn to flee, I was surrounded. One of the men pulled me off my horse. He and his men tied me behind him on his horse. They grabbed my horse's reins. Then we all took off galloping to the northwest to get far away from the battle. We traveled until nightfall. By the hour of the drum, we were in sight of what seemed to be a prosperous farm. The men were grumbling, so their leader, whose name I later learned was Ma Xun, gave in to them.

"All right," he said. "We will stay at that farmhouse tonight."

When we galloped into the yard, the couple who owned the farm were completely overwhelmed. They bent and *kowtowed* as they opened the door. Fear was etched in their faces.

Ma snapped at them. "Food and wine for my men. Feed our horses. Warm the fire---the night is chill. And find a safe place to keep this prisoner." He pointed to me.

The farmer and his wife nodded. Pale with fright, they scurried around to obey Ma's orders while their servants prepared food. When they had done what he wanted, they pointed out a vegetable cellar where I could be kept.

"Go," Ma shouted to the farmer. "And take your servants with you."

Without protest, they hurried out into the chilly night, relieved to escape.

I was pulled into the house and roughly thrown into the cellar. The wooden door was slammed and bolted. The smell of the damp earth along with the smell of rotting vegetables made me gag. I felt as though I was already dead and buried. I was panicky and was breathing rapidly. As my eyes adjusted, I saw minute cracks in the door. At least I wasn't going to be smothered right away. I had trouble stilling my mind. Images of women, who had been buried alive with their husbands when they died, kept rising up in my mind. I hoped to see the morning sun again.

CHAPTER 2

I could hear the muffled noises of the men. They had food and had discovered the family's wine stock. I fell asleep from exhaustion. Suddenly, light struck my face. Several pairs of hands pulled me roughly through the opening and led me to the center of the main room. Ma circled around me.

"We must move on soon. Wu has temporarily beaten back our army. You are a nuisance and a difficulty. We need to join our army in Peking. What should I do with you?"

"Well, Wu will soon be looking for me. And his wrath will be formidable."

Ma slapped my face; I fell to the floor.

"Your general will soon be on his knees when we have regrouped in Peking. Li Zicheng will be the new emperor of China.

I laughed sarcastically. "Li? What a joke, ruler of China?" At that moment, I suspected that I would be killed. "Li, and the likes of you? He is a pretentious postal clerk and a cruel brute who tortures and kills old men. And he has to pay dearly for the loyalty of a ragtag bunch of soldiers like you—you are too stupid to rule even the smallest village, and so is he."

Ma flicked his knife across my face. I could feel blood at the corner of my mouth. He looked down at me with menace. Then he turned slowly toward his men.

"We know what Wu likes. We can all sample the favors of Wu's whore."

He surveyed the room quickly, until his eyes rested on the family altar. He dragged it to the center of the room.

"This will do. It is too high but we can find a mounting box."

At this, his men raised their drinks with a roar of shouting. He pointed to several of his men.

"Lift her up here." Ma found some ropes and pull cords used to summon servants. "These will do quite well," he said.

His men tied my hands together above my head and attached the cord to the end piece of the altar. Ma nodded in satisfaction. "It will be more interesting to leave her legs free. Her movements should be stimulating."

Again, everyone laughed. Ma was the first to mount me.

"Now, if ever," I thought, "I need to use Master Yang's lessons. I must make my mind leave this place." I was aware of my body fighting, but my mind tried for detachment. "It will end... It will end," I repeated to myself like a mantra.

The wine was having its effect so that some of the men were unable to perform.

Others were even lying on the floor in a stupor. The pain on the side of my face where Ma had cut me with his knife was beginning to throb, and I could feel blood running between my legs. I moved my head slowly, trying to focus on the room. Again, Ma was the first person I saw. I could see that he was turning something over in his mind.

He faced his men. "Do we have a good calligrapher here?"

Several of the men thrust a young man forward. He wasn't dressed like a soldier. I wondered how he came to be with this group. Ma put his arm around the young man's shoulder and walked him towards me talking softly into his ear as they came. The young man shrank and tried to turn away. He shook his head no vigorously. Ma hissed into his ear. Then Ma turned to face the rest of the room.

"Wu and his whore believe that we are an army of ignorant peasants. We will send him a message in elegant calligraphy."

Although no one understood his meaning, there was a general shout of agreement. Ma turned to the young man.

"You won't fail me, will you?" Then he said, "Our honor and your life are at stake. If you don't do this, I will kill you and the woman now. Why, your hands are shaking. Someone bring him a drink to calm him."

Several men rushed forward with wine. Ma commanded, "Drink."

The boy drank, choked and then wiped his mouth with the back of his hand. He straightened and approached me hesitantly, all the while carefully avoiding my eyes. The brazier on which the meats had been cooked still burned hot with charcoal. Ma moved it closer to me. He found a long thin blade and heated it until it was glowing hot. He motioned for several soldiers to hold my legs and my waist.

"Absolutely tight," he said. "If she moves, the calligraphy will be ruined." He came to stand by my head and hissed into my ear, "Wu's whore."

I understood. I was to be branded on my belly. "Don't think," I said to myself. "Let your mind take you away!" But the smell of my own burning flesh nauseated me and I began to vomit.

"Hold her tightly," Ma roared.

Salt and bile were rising in my mouth. My chest was heaving. "Count the strokes," I told myself. "Seven strokes for Wu ... oh, too many!" At that point, I must have lost consciousness. It was much later when I awoke. Men were hurriedly packing some of the landowner's possessions which they thought might be valuable. The young man who had done the calligraphy was sitting on a bench next to me with tears running silently down his face.

Ma shot him a contemptuous look as he passed by. "So sensitive," he sneered, "possibly you will not mind dying for her." The man looked at him blankly.

Ma said, "I will not kill her. Wu no doubt will. I'll send her back to him as a gift. I would like to see his face when he sets eyes upon her now. It will slow him down certainly. And think of his loss of face!" Ma leaned back at the waist roaring with laughter at his own cleverness.

"But she can't ride like this," protested the young man.

"On the contrary, we will tie her to the horse. I have heard rumors that she is a very good horsewoman. We can put a white cloth under her to catch the blood and draw Wu's attention to her slight spoilage, but she must remain unclothed so that all can admire your handiwork. Of course you will need to guide her. Wu will undoubtedly kill you both."

The young man looked into my eyes for the first time. "Yes," he said, "I should be the one to go with her."

Ma responded loudly, "Ah. So brave … Fool!"

I was tied on the horse. The men gawked and shouted obscenities at me.

I was determined not to give them the satisfaction of seeing my weakness. Although I had nothing on, I sat as straight as I could astride the horse, while the young man rode beside me and guided my horse.

"I can't ask you to forgive me," he said. "But let me serve you as long as we live, and if the need comes, I will give my life for you."

I couldn't hate him. If he hadn't been the one, then it would have meant his death and another would have been found to do what he had done. As soon as we were out of sight of Ma's troops and beyond the city, he stopped the horses. Taking off his tunic, he arranged it gently around my shoulders. He untied my hands and massaged the feeling back into them.

"Lean on the horse's neck and rest if you can."

I was grateful to collapse.

"What will happen to us when your general sees what has been done to you?"

I knew he was trying to prepare his mind for torture or death.

"I don't know. He is fond of me, but I still don't know his heart when he is most angry," I replied, "We must expect anything."

I, too, was going through all the hells my imagination could conceive of. Such a loss of face would be an immense effrontery to a man of Wu's pride. Would he blame me? He might despise me now that I was mutilated. I couldn't predict his reaction.

We traveled through the rest of the night. Just when I thought I could not stand another movement of the horse, we saw the lights of Wu's camp in the valley below. A sentry came running out.

"I am Bourtai, Wu's concubine, with an escort."

The sentry looked at me closely and then began to run to Wu's quarters. Within minutes, Wu was dashing up the hill towards me. Several of his men followed. When he reached me, he had a look of joy on his face which immediately turned to one of alarm when he saw my condition.

I returned his gaze as levelly as I could. "My Lord," I said, "I have come back to you."

Wu's men roughly dragged the young man from his horse.

"No," I shouted. "He has helped me. Don't hurt him."

Then everything began to swim in front of my eyes and I slid from the horse into Wu's arms. I was soon lying in his tent. He shouted for his physician, a basin of water and some cloths. It was not the physician who bathed me, but Wu, himself. He gently pulled my matted hair from my cheek where Ma had cut me with his knife.

"The man who did this will suffer a thousand deaths for what he has done," he said through clenched teeth. He removed the coverlet and saw the branding. His face blanched. Then he gasped. He closed his eyes for a moment. "No!" he screamed. He knocked over the stool he was sitting on. Taking in ragged gulps of air, he rushed to a nearby table and began to pound his fist against it repeatedly. By the time he had calmed down, his physician had arrived. He gave me a draft of a strong sedative.

When Wu returned to my side I said, "A mirror, please," stretching out my hand.

"Not now. You must sleep. It will heal. It will be fine." Wu held my hand tightly.

The physician sprinkled a fine dust of healing powder over my belly and my cheek. Then he gave me a sleeping draft and something for the pain. I began to cry. I started to float in and out of consciousness as the physician packed my groin to stop the bleeding. Soon warmth coursed through my body. The pain was receding, and I felt like I was rising on a cushion of clouds like the clouds Wu and

I had watched on the plains. My only memories of that night are of sometimes waking momentarily from a deep sleep to hear eerie, almost human-sounding howls of some strange animal echoing across the valley. I was told later that Wu had galloped back and forth in the hills shouting and cursing like a madman. His father, his concubine and now me—he must have hit his breaking point.

When he came to my bedside in the morning, there was no trace of the madman. Instead, his face was set in determination. "I must leave you in camp for a while. I promise; this time you will be safe. If I don't follow the band of men who did this, I may lose them. You must regain your strength. In a few days when you are better, you can follow our army in a sedan chair which I will arrange for you."

"And the young man?" I asked.

Wu answered. "He is not a man; he is a eunuch who was taken from the Forbidden City to serve Ma's men as a slave. He has been badly used also. If you like, he can be your personal servant."

"Yes, I would like that."

He kissed my forehead lightly, then turned and walked away. My heart fell at the simple goodbye; however, he turned again before he left and met my eyes. "Remember," he said. "You are still my beautiful horsewoman."

The next few days were unusual for the area near Peking. Instead of the wind which usually blew dust over everything, the days were calm and still. The eunuch would carry me outside where I could sit in the sun and watch the sky. He told me his name was Feng Xianfu.

He said, "My family was so large and so poor that I was sent to become a eunuch." The emperor had paid his family for him. Supposedly he would have a better life at court, but he was captured by Li's men when they entered Peking.

We talked about what was happening in China. "The people looked to the emperor like a father," Feng said. "They have been loyal, but things have only gotten worse. The emperor took land from the peasants and gave it to the gentry as favors. I heard rumors that even his troops had not been paid recently, yet he lived in splendor inside his wall of dreams."

"Yes, that's also what Wu has told me. For the majority of the people, their greatest desire has always been for stability and enough to eat. They care little for politics."

As I recovered from what Ma and his men did to me, I thought back to the events that resulted in my capture. As a younger girl, I was confident that I would always have an easy time in the world. How naïve I was. It would take me a while to recapture my strength and my confidence. I thought about my early life which led up to this point. I re-lived it in my mind.

CHAPTER 3

I am Bourtai of the Manchus. Although the woman for whom I am named lived hundreds of years ago, her legend is still fresh in the minds of my people. She was a remarkable woman of great power. As the wife of Ghenghis Khan, she administered the workings of his confederation of Mongol tribes while he was away on his many travels of conquest. She held the center for him with consistent force and wisdom as he gathered more and more lands and people under his rule.

My grandmother, Mamu, never tired of telling me stories about Bourtai and also about Empress Wu who was the only female ruler of China. Mamu urged me to emulate their cleverness.

She said, "You may never have their power, but you can achieve wisdom and knowledge which will help you greatly throughout your life."

My education was extensive for a woman. Now, my life spread out before me; nevertheless, I feared that men would determine its course. This is the way it is for all women. We can only hope to be lucky, wise and clever. My new life began abruptly.

I first saw General Wu San Gui one day as I was sitting in the courtyard of our palace. He, along with Dorgon and another man who did not look either Chinese or Manchu, paced the grounds in intense conversation.

Our Manchu men affect a hairstyle in which they shave the fronts and tops of their heads leaving a long braid hanging down their backs. This Chinese general wore his hair loosely and his head was not shaved. Instead, his hair hung down in splendid black waves. I couldn't help but stare. For a moment he caught my eyes. His were an intense black. He seemed slightly amused by my interest in him. His nose was straight and strong, and he moved with a confident bearing that was compelling. I blushed and hurriedly looked at the ground, but I had memorized his face, the face that would remain in my mind throughout my life. Later, I learned that the third man was Wu's aide, Xi Chu. He was a Uigher from the far west. His nose was long and hooked and his skin was darker than ours. His eyes were round and more pronounced. They were a strange icy blue. From the moment I first saw him I did not like him. He seemed sinister to me.

And of General Wu San Gui, what can I tell about him after all these year? While many call him traitor, and eventually double traitor, I came to call him lover. His life and mine were woven and rewoven for both good and ill.

My life up to that point of seeing Wu for the first time had been full and exciting, but a bit protected. I lived in the palace compound with Mamu in a separate palace apartment. There I grew up and discovered much about myself and the world. I also learned much about my past and probable future. I had always thought that Mamu was my mother, but one morning, in my tenth year, she startled me by saying, "Child, it is time that you know I am not your mother." I listened in silence as she continued. "Your mother is my daughter. She is a beauty and has a quick mind. I suppose that is why she was chosen."

"Chosen, chosen for what?" I cried, "Why isn't she here with me? Didn't she love me?"

I couldn't imagine a mother who would leave her child. Mamu tried to soothe me.

She explained, "You were her life, but she was forced to do something of great value for our clan. After your father died in battle, she was married to the leader of another clan in order to tie our two clans together. At that time, Nurhachi was our Grand Khan. He chose her. She had to obey, but she wept bitterly when she left you. But she did know that I would be like a mother to you."

I turned this new information over in my mind. "So her life was decided by men?"

"Yes," Mamu answered, "women have always been like game pieces in the eyes of men. Our only value is in how we are used. You, too, are valuable like your mother was. You are being educated for some reason, but I don't know what Dorgon will choose for you. Because of our khan's death last year, Dorgon, as the regent for Fulin the child who will be our next khan, will decide what is to happen to you. I can only give you all my love while there is still time."

She pulled me into her arms, and I could feel her body shake. Her tears fell onto my arm. How could I be nothing, yet also be a person of value?

Mamu explained our history. "Our Jurchen leaders had great territorial ambitions. When Nurhachi proclaimed himself Grand Khan, many smaller clans joined us after battles, by shifting loyalties or by establishing marriages that bound the clans together. Our united peoples took the name of Manchus from the word *Mukden* that means social cooperation. Nurhachi invaded the Chinese territories in Liaodong south of us. He brought back many Chinese prisoners who were useful in a number of ways, such as building cannons or organizing our new confederation into a powerful nation. Nurhachi was my older brother, so I was given this palace compound. When Nurhachi died, his son, Abahai, succeeded him. Now with Abahai's recent death, Dorgon has become regent for Fulin, our new child khan. Dorgon takes his responsibilities seriously. So far, he hasn't tried to usurp power from our child leader."

Mamu said that Dorgon told her I would soon be of an age where I would be important to our people. I feared that becoming older meant great changes, perhaps changes like those which took my mother away. I was frightened. Still, I had many advantages. As a child, although I didn't realize it, I was spoiled. My clothes were fine. My outdoor boots were made of intricately decorated leather. My best garments had sable or fox fur trimmings. My tutor taught me to read and write Mongolian and Mandarin. He schooled me well in our own Manchu language. He also taught me in history and mathematics.

Sometime after Nurhachi became khan, he moved our capital to Mukden (later known as Shenyang) where he built an imposing palace. It was here that Mamu and I lived. People compared the palace to the Forbidden City in Peking, yet it was much smaller. It was here in a side courtyard that I received many of my lessons. And it was here that I met my new teacher Master Yang. He was to become my lifelong friend and my Buddhist master. His name was Yang Shuzheng.

I was sent into the courtyard to meet this person. As I entered the courtyard, I saw a man sitting motionless on a bench. The sun shone on him. On his nose a fly sat also motionless. I watched. I expected the man to swat the fly away at any moment. It felt like an eternity had passed. Finally, a cramp in my leg pushed me to walk forward.

"What are you doing?" I asked.

He replied, "I am meditating. What are you doing?"

"I am watching you meditate," I said.

"That is most impolite," he said, "and look, now you have disturbed the fly."

I stared at him puzzled. "How do you meditate? And why?"

He looked me up and down. He rose and circled me. I tried to remain as still as the fly.

"How would you like to learn to meditate?"

I was amazed. "You can teach me that?"

"No, I can't teach you anything, but I can help you learn what you want to learn. Consider this, come here tomorrow at this same time if you want to begin."

I *kowtowed* to him. Then I turned and ran without speaking. My head was buzzing. I could not form solid thoughts. Indeed, if I learned how to meditate that would be wonderful. The next morning I returned.

Before Master Yang could speak I asked, "Who are you?"

He looked surprised. He said, "I am a Buddhist monk."

"Buddhist," I said, "What is that?"

"Ah…well, it is somewhat difficult to explain. We Buddhists believe that the Buddha was a very wise and compassionate man who became so good that he was able to leave this world and go to *Nirvana.*"

"Where is *Nirvana?* Is it better than being here?"

He replied, "It is no place and every place."

I frowned, "I don't understand."

"Let me try to explain. *Nirvana* is the end of the pain and suffering we experience in life. In one sense it is beyond this life, but in another sense it is right here in the midst of life. It is a state of mind in which we rise above the pain and suffering and put an end to the selfishness and grasping on to life which so often produces our pain and suffering."

I think I understood what he was saying, but I was still puzzled. Trying to get my mind to think the way he thought made me dizzy.

He noticed my puzzlement and said, "Have you heard of Kuan Yin?"

I nodded. "My grandmother prays to Kuan Yin. She is a powerful goddess who does not have children, but gives special help to mothers."

He replied, "We Buddhists know her as a *bodhisattva.* Like the Buddha she is so good that she could leave the earth and go to *Nirvana.*"

"Well, if *Nirvana* is so wonderful, why doesn't she go there?"

He became thoughtful for a moment. "Because she can't bear the suffering of the people she sees. She has vowed to stay on earth to help until there is no more suffering. Then she will go."

I just looked at him. "You mean all the suffering in the whole land? That is silly. That will never happen."

Master Yang gave a knowing smile, but his eyes were sad. "You may be right, but I choose to hope. Ah, yes, I must hope."

I turned and ran without speaking. My head buzzed with things I didn't understand; however, I was determined to learn. Before this, I listened to adults talk about gods, but I never tried to decide just what I believed. I realized that I was very sheltered. Now, it was time for me to consider the world outside.

The next morning I returned for more instructions. Master Yang was sitting on the same bench with a table in front of him. On the table lay pieces of very thin rice paper. He was making strong, bold lines with a brush and ink on one of the pieces. The lines leapt into a life of their own. I thought they were especially beautiful because they were a mystery I didn't understand.

Master Yang laid his brush down and looked up with a smile. "I was expecting you. You are early too. This is a good sign. So you want to learn to meditate?"

"Yes," I stammered. "No, first I want to learn their meanings." I pointed to his paper.

His face crinkled into a grin. "A wise answer and a bold one also. Come, sit. Rest your wrist flat on the table and hold the brush upright between these fingers." He demonstrated. "Now the brush is part of your arm. Relax and I will guide your arm."

He swept my hand from left to right. Then he lifted the brush above the center of the horizontal stroke and swept it down to the left in an arc. Finally, he added another arc to the right, intersecting the horizontal stroke. Like magic a character appeared.

"Ha, you see? You can write. This is *da* 'big'. Watch me." He made the character again and again. "Now, you do it."

I did as he said. My characters looked wobbly compared to his bold strokes.

He said, "It is not easy. You will learn only 'big' today. Tomorrow is 'small' day."

I spent the next few hours writing *da-da-da* until my arm and hand were numb. When I went home for an afternoon nap, I fell into bed exhausted with the characters swimming in front of my eyes.

"I will learn to write the Chinese way," I whispered to myself with determination.

The next morning, I was earlier for my lessons than the day before.

"Ah, my eager pupil, and what shall I call you?"

"Bourtai, just Bourtai is how I am known."

"I have heard of a Bourtai, but I am sure she did not look like you."

For the following two years, I spent every morning with Master Yang learning to read and write. I learned about Buddhist thought,

Daoist thought and even about Confucianism. But most importantly I learned how to meditate or as Master Yang said 'concentrate'. One day as I practiced concentrating, I heard a piercing cry from outside the walls of the enclosure. My eyes popped open.

"What is the world like outside?" I demanded.

Master Yang sighed, "So much for meditating---the world? It is less orderly and harmonious but often more interesting. It can be uglier than you can possibly imagine, but nevertheless strikingly beautiful. Ultimately it has a sameness because all people are basically alike. See for yourself. Go outside alone, but be very careful."

"But that is not permitted. I sometimes go outside our walls, but I must stay with a hunting party where someone can watch me. Or I go out with our servant, Girtin."

Master Yang gave me an intense look. "I know a great deal about you. Besides being quick and beautiful, you are also headstrong. You listen in on the men's councils like a mouse in a corner. Your curiosity is greater than your fear."

I was shocked, "How do you know all that?"

"I have survived by being a quiet man, but I observe well. Do you think I don't watch what you do?"

"Then why do you teach me if I am so headstrong?"

"I was asked to teach you by Abahai and then by Dorgon after Abahai died. It is the right thing to do. It would be a shame to waste your intelligence. You will make a fine tribute gift if Dorgon needs one."

This idea frightened me.

Master Yang chuckled and looked down.

"What is the joke?" I replied in a huff.

"Possibly it is the feet," he said, "Yours are not to the Chinese liking. The learned Chinese physicians believe that foot binding greatly enhances men's pleasure. Possibly foot binding increases the folds in the brain."

I was taken aback at what he said. He was so open with me! I looked at him a moment until I realized he believed in neither possibility. I couldn't keep from laughing.

We Manchu women never bound our feet. I found it sad to think of Chinese women tottering around on tiny painful feet that often hurt so badly that they could travel much less than a fifth of a *li* at most.

"I understand that you have also learned to dance," he said.

I gasped, "How do you know that I can dance?"

"No one told me. I saw you in the dancers' tent."

I knew what he meant by referring to the dancers' tent. One day, our servant, Girten and I visited the market outside the palace. This was a rare event for me. Mamu always cautioned Girten to keep close watch over me. The market was lively, especially with the news that a caravan had come into Mukden from the west on the silk road. It brought many wonders. I formed a vision in my head of the silk road. What color was it? Did it extend thousands of *lis* to the northwest? Why and how could anyone make a road that long? I questioned Girten.

"No, you silly girl. The road is not made of silk, but traders come from far away to get Chinese silk to sell back in their homelands. They, in turn, bring us spices that they trade for the silks. That is why it is called the silk road."

I felt very foolish, but I was determined to learn more. I was glad that it was only Girten who heard my questions. All the people in the market were gaping at one of the marvelous animals that was with the caravan. It was called a giraffe. I thought maybe that was what the *quilins* in our fairy stories looked like, but it was uglier than a *quilin* should be. Later that night, I slipped out as I had before to spy on our leaders in their councils. Because it was inside the palace grounds, Girten didn't scold me, although, she was supposed to be making sure that she knew what I was doing. I always reported any news I gathered back to her.

Again, I went to a place where I could see through a crack into the hall while the men gathered in the council room. As usual, they were arguing, drinking and shouting. What occurred next was a marvel. Three women came into the center of the gathering and a hush fell. The women had almost nothing on except skirts of very thin silk of a kind that didn't come from Manchuria. Glittering gold disks covered their breast; they had bells on their ankles and small gold disks on their fingers. They began to sway and make circles with their hips in a way that most women would never dream of doing. The men started clapping their hands to the beat of the disks. The dancers just smiled, their eyes flashing as they danced even faster than before.

I was entranced. The dancers were so graceful. I had to know more. I wanted to find out where they were staying. I guessed that they were on the palace grounds somewhere. And I was right.

After exploring, I discovered a makeshift tent at the farthest corner of the palace walls. I could hear bells tinkling and the soft cadence of tapping disks. I moved to see these women up closer. They were beautiful. I moved even closer to the tent, when one of the dancers whirling near the opening jumped out and grabbed my wrist. She pulled me into the middle of the tent. I gave a small yelp, but she was too strong. She held me there. The others started laughing. If I were a rabbit, I would have scuttled away. However, the women seemed kind. They touched me lightly and examined my clothes. One even hugged me. Then they tried to talk with me by making gestures. Finally, I understood that they were asking me if I would like to learn to dance. I did a few skipping steps and nodded yes. My lessons began. I was awkward at first, but I soon found that the movements released something inside of me that I hadn't known was there. Twirling was pure joy. Clanging disks gave me a sense of power. I was certain that the power I felt was something that Manchu women, or even Chinese women never experienced.

The dancers stayed inside the compound for several days. I memorized every movement that I could in those few days. I would have to keep practicing to retain what I already knew. I confided to Girten. She kept my secret. Shortly before the dancers were to leave, Girten and I fashioned small leather purses for each of them. I put Manchu coins inside each purse. These small gifts delighted the women. In return, they gave me a set of finger disks, bells, and a lovely sheer skirt like the ones they danced in. In addition I received a golden top to fit over my breasts. I put these gifts in the bottom of one of my chests. These possessions would be my secret.

I was very embarrassed when I found out that Master Yang knew about my dancing. I must have turned as red as a persimmon.

He merely looked at me and smiled.

"Never be ashamed of anything you learn. Everything will be useful at some time. Remember my child, modesty in a woman is not necessarily the virtue men would have you believe. It is merely a way of making women compliant to the wishes of men. Women, even the most passive, can bring about many changes. You are becoming a woman of value. Make good use of your intelligence and everything you have learned."

"But women are less…less…it has always been so." I was at a loss to explain.

"You are wrong. Women are half of humanity. Remember our study of *yin* and *yang*. Each is half. The world would not work if it were otherwise. Cold/hot, light/dark, men/women; they should be balanced."

I looked at him in wonder. This, indeed, was a new idea to chew on. I was curious to know if he enjoyed the women's dancing. After all, he was a man.

CHAPTER 4

One morning Master Yang said, "It's time for you to practice becoming invisible."

Again he confounded me. "Invisible?" I mouthed stupidly. "How can anyone be truly invisible? Is it magic?"

"No, I don't believe in the 'magic' that some of my fellow practitioners claim to possess. It is just a trick. It is a trick you used before I even met you. I have seen you sitting in a corner like a mouse, all ears, but not moving. No one noticed you. It is only in the minds of others that you can become invisible. This is PRINCIPLE ONE.

PRINCIPLE TWO: Act only in the way others expect you to, at least in their presence.

PRINCIPLE THREE: If necessary, look unexceptional. No fine clothes, cover your head if you can, and be mindful of your walk, nothing elegant. In these ways, you can be unnoticed. I'm afraid it may be difficult for you. You have too much curiosity and too much pride, but you can practice. It may be useful in the future."

I looked at him. "How did you come to be here teaching me? I know that Dorgon requested it."

He chuckled, "Oh I was blown here by the wind. I joined a caravan on the silk-road in order to travel more safely. Far from here, a band of brigands attacked the caravan and captured many of us. I was of no use to them, so they traded me to another tribe farther east. Through a series of trades, I ended here. You might say I was passed along."

I smiled at him. "I'm glad you were passed along."

With his instructions, I grew, I learned to think and meditate, to be visible and almost invisible. My young life was full. I was changing both inside and out.

When I was younger, my chest was like a boy's, but since then, soft mounds had appeared. When I bathed and brushed my nipples lightly with my hand, I felt a pleasurable sensation between my legs; however, I didn't ask Mamu what was happening when I began to bleed. I found rags to catch the blood. After a few days, the bleeding stopped. The bleeding returned the next month and the next until finally, sobbing over my injury, I asked Girten what was wrong with me.

She said, "Nothing is wrong with you. It is a rhythm peculiar to women. It means that you could have a baby. I should have told you. I'm sorry."

I was happy to be a woman now, but I certainly didn't want a baby yet. I wondered what was in store for me. When I listened to women talk, I heard horror stories about men and their rough ways with women.

I was still as curious as ever. I managed to listen in to conversations that I wasn't supposed to hear. At times, a member of our court went to the capital in Peking, probably to deliver tribute. Anyone who went, returned and spoke with awe about the magnificence of the Ming Dynasty. The Forbidden City sounded like a grand dream. I tried to visualize it. I also began to hear rumors about the unrest that was growing in China. I knew our leaders had their eyes on China. In their councils, they salivated with glee like hungry wolves that caught the scent of a weakening prey. The Chinese were divided and ready for revolt. Li Zicheng gathered many disaffected peasants and others into a large peasant army. He intended to overthrow the reigning emperor who was a weak leader. The corruption throughout the emperor's court was rampant.

Li promised the peasants great wealth if they joined him in seizing the throne and occupying Peking. Other peasant armies that had similar aims, were gathered far to the west, but Li's army was, by far, the largest. The Chinese emperor rightly feared the growing powers coming at him from all sides. He also knew about the ambition of the Manchus. Because of this, he sent General Wu San Gui to guard the Shan Hai Guan garrison at the farthest eastern point of the Great Wall which ended at the Bo Hai Gulf.

At that time, our Manchu troops massed on the northern side of the Great Wall; however, the wall itself and the garrison seemed impregnable. A different plan was necessary for the Manchus to have any chance of gaining territory near to China proper. Possibly General Wu, so near with his army guarding the garrison could be the answer. Wu knew Dorgon. Previously, they had communicated.

In April, Li Zicheng and his army of peasant soldiers besieged and overthrew the imperial government of China. The Ming Emperor Xi Zong did not take interest in military maneuvers. Those who knew him, said that he was a peculiar man. He did not spend much time learning to read and write. Rather, he worked on carpentry, crafting many pieces of fine furniture. He was totally out of touch with the peasants in the countryside. When several traitorous eunuchs opened the gate of Peking and, finally, the gates of the Forbidden City to crowds of the peasant army, the Ming Emperor knew he was NO LONGER The Son of Heaven.

The failed emperor killed his family and many of his concubines. Then, when he saw that he couldn't escape, he climbed Coal Hill at the north end of the palace. From this vantage point, he could see his palace and part of his city in flaming ruins. He wrote a message in his own blood: *My virtue is small; therefore I have incurred the anger of heaven, and rebels have captured my capital.* He loosened his sash, and with the help of a retainer, hanged himself from a tree. People who were near said the body swung gently in the light from the inferno of what had once been his splendid city. At the time, I did not know all this; I was to learn about it later.

We were all aware of the tension in Mukden and knew that our army was encamped north of Shan Hai Guan. Most of us believed that our army intended to move into China, but it could not advance through the Great Wall without the help of Wu San Gui. But how could his help be gained?

Then it happened as Mamu predicted. I had become an object of great value. It was not long after I first saw Wu San Gui that Dorgon gave me to Wu as a bribe; however, the bribe was unnecessary. Wu's mind was made up before I was given to him. I was just an encumbrance in his drive for revenge for his father's torture and death and the fact that his favorite concubine was given to one of Li's generals.

When Dorgon presented me to Wu, Wu barely glanced at me. Later, he turned on me with a sarcastic growl saying, "What am I to do with you?" His words were devastating to me. I remembered well my attraction toward him that day in the palace courtyard.

Our second meeting was not what I dreamed of. "I will be no bother," I said, "I can ride a horse as fast and as long as any of your men. I can also ride a reindeer," I added in a near whisper.

"Well, I'm sorry I have no reindeer to provide for you," he answered in a gruff voice.

His sarcasm was stinging. I fought to keep tears from coming to my eyes.

"Come," he shouted as he waved his hand to one of his men. "See that she is taken care of. We wouldn't want to insult our new allies by not accepting their gift."

The soldier hurriedly pushed me forward toward the tents. Dorgon provided me a large yurt which was erected for me beside Wu's tent to ensure my safety. The soldiers brought my trunks in. I was given some bedding, then abruptly left alone. Sometime later, a hand thrust food into the yurt. For the rest of the night I could concentrate only on my apprehensions. I wasn't sure what was expected of me.

In the morning, one of Wu's lieutenants named Long Qiong brought me a large morning meal. He said, "I am also a Manchu. I am assigned to Wu by Dorgon to ensure that Wu keeps his agreement."

Long Qiong would also become Wu's close retainer like Xi Chu was. It was, however, Long's honesty and integrity which would have a much different influence from that of Xi Chu's.

Meals came regularly, but I was still alone. I wanted to look for one of the scrolls in my trunk, but hesitated to ask for a lantern for night reading. Throughout the next day, I could hear much discussion in Wu's tent; I was not brave enough to do my usual eavesdropping. Finally, toward evening, the flap of my yurt was pulled back. Wu stood outside holding two horses. One was large, and the other was a small Mongolian.

"Come," he said, "I want to see if you can keep up with my army."

My spirits bounded. I jumped barebacked on the Mongolian horse and dug my heels into its flanks. Wu took off at a gallop. Wu was right beside me as we raced through the fields beyond the encampment. I was determined to prove myself. We rode for over an hour. Then Wu held up his hand to halt me.

"All right. I believe you. We should walk the horses back to let them cool down. What else can you do?" he asked.

Words came tumbling out of my mouth. "I could write your dispatches in either Manchu or *putonghua*. I can do sums. I can play the *erhu*. I can dance. I can…I could be your concubine," I added a bit hesitantly.

"I have concubines!"

Ah yes, I thought. Even in Manchuria, we heard about his beautiful concubine, Chen Yuan Yuan. I quickly tried to change the topic by asking about the situation in Peking. "I have heard rumors about all the destruction that is taking place." But I seemed to get myself in more trouble with my questions.

Wu glanced at me with obvious annoyance. He said, "I was told that you are bold for a woman."

I tried to make amends; instead, I merely blathered on.

"Forgive me for being so curious," I said, "I understand now why you are joining Dorgon."

He just nodded his head curtly in acknowledgment. "We might ride again tomorrow evening. It is good practice for what will be a hard journey to the capital."

I answered softly, "Yes, I would like that."

The evening rides became a habit. I felt totally free. When we walked the horses back to the paddock, I told Wu about some of the things that Master Yang taught me. I told him that Master Yang even insisted that I read Sun Tzu's *The Art of War.*

This astonished him. "Why would your Buddhist master have you read such a non-Buddhist treatise?"

I responded, "It is true that Master Yang doesn't believe in war, but he believes that wars will continue. He thought that understanding the principles of Sun Tzu's ideas could be important even for an observer. Some of the things Sun Tzu said are ones I will always remember. He said that weapons are ominous tools to be used only when there is no alternative. He also talked about the cost of war to the nation and to its peoples. A leader should take this into account. But most importantly he declared that warfare was to know the mind of the enemy---to undermine his confidence and muddle his thoughts. He also said, 'No country has ever benefited from a protracted war. The expert commander strikes only when the situation assures victory.'"

Blathering again! I realized that I was behaving like a bragging upstart to be talking about warfare with a famous general.

Wu looked bemused by my conceit. "My, you are full of your learning," he said. "I see that you have learned your lessons like a prattling parrot. If you can spare me your lectures, we can meet again tomorrow evening to practice our riding. It will amuse me after plotting strategies the whole day."

We continued our evening rides; I learned to hold my tongue. I realized then that I was often impossibly full of myself. As we walked back to cool off the horses, we talked about all manner of things that didn't concern Wu's military calculations. I imagined that I was coming to know his mind. I was truly infatuated. Earlier, I often dreamed of the handsome man I saw in our courtyard. His image became permanently fixed in my head. Now, here he was with me! I studied him closely. I could not imagine a more handsome man. His cheekbones were high; his straight, narrow nose was not like those of the *han* Chinese; his brows rose in almost straight diagonal lines toward his full mane of ink black hair. His face often looked stern, but I imagined a hidden gentleness, at least towards me. This image of him is perhaps how I wanted him to be. My fantasies were about the outer shell. Now, I was trying to understand the actual person.

When we were alone, we talked about our beliefs. He scoffed at the idea of an afterlife. He had no use for the idea of gods or other superstitions. He adhered to the Confucian principle of an hierarchical order to society, while I believed more in compassion and had hope for something better for our people. He laughed at my naiveté.

We even talked about our childhoods. He told me about the strong influence his father had on him. His father was also a famous military general. During his stay in the far west of China, he developed a strong attraction to a Uigher woman. They had a child, Xi Chu. Wu's father expected Wu to take care of his half-brother and promote him. So, that was why Xi Chu was important in Wu's army. I had wondered about him.

I never knew my father. He died in battle shortly after I was conceived. I looked up to my grand-uncle because of his power, but there was no intimacy between us. He was just a passing stranger. I really wasn't familiar with men's ways. Wu seemed to show more interest in me now that we had our evening talks. A male companion was a wonderful novelty for me.

Many evenings we raced across the plains on our horses. One evening when we were out, the sun was just disappearing behind the distant hills. It cast a soft glow on the tall grasses and spread a shimmering glaze on everything. We were taking our horses out of the paddock. I began to cry. Wu looked mystified and concerned.

"What is the matter?" he asked.

I felt foolish. "It is just so beautiful. I think of my grandmother who will spend her whole life behind palace walls, and I realize how lucky I am."

"I am lucky also," he said. "You are turning out to be not only pleasing but also interesting." With that he grinned and slapped my horse on the rump. "Let's ride," he said.

We took off weaving around in circles and crazy loops. Our yells echoed in the hills as we rode. Suddenly, Wu swept beside me and pulled me onto his horse. Then he reined in his horse to an abrupt halt and we tumbled into the grass. I trembled. I didn't know what to expect. The cautionary tales of the palace women flashed through my mind.

Wu knelt between my legs. Pulling my garments up quickly and just as rapidly removing my trousers, he paused to look at me.

"Lovely," he whispered. His words pleased me despite my fears. He lowered himself over me and entered me slowly. I felt quick convulsions of pain. Then, amazingly, I was contracting against him.

"Ah, ah," he shuddered and remained still for a moment.

I could feel my own pulsations inside of me. He wrapped his arms around me and rolled over so that I was on top of him.

"Sit up, my good horsewoman," he laughed. "I am your wild Mongolian horse. You must tame me."

With that, he began thrusting against me. In seconds I was responding, pounding against him as though I was riding across the plains. I felt a power I had never known before. I thought, "My horse is going so fast we both shall die."

Wu arched his back and froze for a second, moaning. I felt as though a shock had coursed through my body. I contracted violently against him in spasms and collapsed on his chest. He began stroking my hair.

"Excellent, excellent horsewoman," he whispered.

I was exuberant. I felt strong and sure of myself. I knew one thing. I was Wu's for either heaven or hell. I didn't know that hell would come to me very soon.

During those incredible evenings, we raced our horses across the plains until I was near exhaustion. At times, we would play at being opposing armies as we rode rapidly toward each other. At the last moment, one of us would feint to the right or left to elude our opponent. Again, Wu would catch me, and once again, we would tumble into the high grass. We rolled and fought each other hitting in mock anger. Then we were still. To tease me, Wu would move very slowly until he was on top of me. I felt dizzy from the efforts of the pursuit, but my energy returned. The patterns of the swiftly moving clouds overhead were soon obscured by Wu's hair as it fell on either side of me. I could see only the intensity of his eyes and feel the heat in my groin. If I could put pebbles on one side of a pair of scales as symbols of happiness, the joyful side would tip to the ground. This frightened me, for I remembered Master Yang's lessons and his emphasis upon the balance of life. But at that moment, I felt that I was the most fortunate woman in the world.

When we were satiated, Wu lay beside me as we watched the rolling clouds darken into night.

"Such an accomplished horsewoman," he said.

"How can I be a horsewoman when the horse is on top of me?"

"That happens to the best of us," he replied. "When the horse goes down we must just relax and roll with it. My horse is essential to me, but you are becoming important to me also."

To our side, I saw our horses looking at us with mild curiosity as they grazed a small distance away.

"Poor beasts," Wu said as he kissed my ear, "never to know such passion!"

Wu had always prided himself on being accessible to his men. Despite our growing affection, he wanted to be available to his lieutenants. He had another small tent set up next to my yurt for my own personal bodyguard to sleep in. Thus Wu's men knew they could approach him in his own tent at any time he was there; however, he did spend some evenings with me. His men were instructed to interrupt him only with urgent dispatches concerning the movement of Li's troops.

When Wu was a Ming Dynasty general, the Ming Emperor made him an Earl of the Realm. He received many valuable gifts at that time. Now, with his intention to join with the Manchu army, he found these gifts particularly troubling. He told me about these feelings, so I suggested that he give those gifts to his most faithful lieutenants.

I said, "Surely you will be rewarded with similar gifts and titles by Dorgon and the Manchus. Those you can keep without regret."

He was satisfied with my suggestion.

The next day Wu said, "Li Zicheng has left Peking and is coming to meet my army. It will be a difficult battle. I'm counting on Dorgon for the help he promised."

Wu reiterated his appeal to Dorgon who was about 60 *li* north of Shan Hai Guan.

Dorgon immediately ordered his troops to march south. They covered the distance in twenty hours, but they were too exhausted to engage in battle right away.

Wu said to me, "We may have only one more evening together for a while. I will be busy all day but wait supper for me. I'll have the cooks prepare special dishes for tonight. We'll be moving against Li's army soon. This may be our last night together for some time."

I tried to nap so that I would be fresh for the evening, but I was too agitated to sleep. I hadn't made a proper farewell to Mamu, Girten and Master Yang. Wu would soon be too occupied with fighting to spend any time with me. I dreaded the loneliness to come. My body was just getting used to the surprising new creature who inhabited it. This new being demanded that its skin be stroked and its needs be met. I had learned the feel of my lover's skin. Now, I must store strong memories to sustain me in the future.

I washed and dressed myself in anticipation of the evening. Whenever my hands brushed my body I remembered the feel of Wu touching me. It gave me shivers of delight. Skin is such a remarkable gift!

Wu finally appeared at the doorway of my yurt. I had worked myself to such a feverish pitch that I could barely contain myself as the servants filed in with the various dishes. I remained absolutely still. Their incredible slowness was agonizing. At last they left. I launched myself at Wu with a cry that I didn't recognize as my own. I wrapped my arms around his neck and encircled his waist with my legs. He staggered under the weight of my sudden attack. He looked stunned. Then, with a slow smile he said, "So this is the way it is to be tonight?"

I pressed upward with all my strength. "Please…now…please?"

We performed a frenzied dance, ecstatic, but exhausting. My mind flew away from my body. When I came back into myself, I was lying there soaked with sweat.

"Perfect," he said. He gave me a wry look. "Now can we eat? I seem to be hungry."

I was suddenly embarrassed. "Forgive me." I jumped up to get a platter of sliced duck which at that moment looked delectably good to me too. Wu put a sliver of glazed duck on his tongue. He then pulled it into his mouth in the same way a snake would.

"Incomparable," he sighed, "the duck and the appetizer. Never apologize for passion my dear; apologize only for lack of passion. Tomorrow I engage in a different kind of passion. Li Zicheng is coming near with his army to meet us."

I jumped to my feet. "Then I must pack at once. I'll take only what I can carry on my horse."

"No, no," he said pulling me into his arms. "Tomorrow must not spoil tonight. I will send you with some guards to take you safely away from the battlefield. When it is over, you can travel with my army to see our triumphant entry into Peking."

He rolled toward me again. "The duck was superb. Let's see if we can repeat what we just did."

I said, "I have merely one request. I want to watch the battle from the nearby hill. It will be safe enough. Large rocks are sitting there in front of a copse of trees. Surely it will be a good hiding place. Please say that I can do that." I stroked his cheek.

He considered for a minute. "All right, I'll send some guards with you, but you must leave for Shan Hai Guan at once if the battle begins to turn in Li's favor." Then he laughed, "That is not a possibility. We will fill the plain with Li's fallen soldiers." He looked at me appraisingly. "I thought you were a peace loving woman who followed your Buddhist teacher."

"I know I am inconsistent. I don't like the idea of war, but I do like a very special warrior. I want to see him demonstrate his skills. Besides, the thought of Li and his ruffians makes me angry enough to fight too."

Wu laughed again and said, "I will put on a very spirited battle for you to watch."

CHAPTER 5

As I was recovering after the battle and the horrible events which followed, I spent much time with Feng. We played chess. I had to coach him on this. We made up word games and riddles and, in general, tried to ignore the world. We talked about ourselves and began to feel like brother and sister.

"Tell me about your general," Feng said. "Is he so different from other men? I'm amazed to still be alive."

"Well, about Wu," I smiled. "How shall I describe him? To me he seems the most wonderful of men. I suppose he is taller than most because he was born in Liaodong where the men are taller than the *han* Chinese. He looks more like a Manchu with his high cheek bones and his long thin nose. He moves with the power and grace of a tiger. Don't you think so?"

Feng laughed. "You speak like a woman in love, but that is just a physical description which I can see for myself. What is he really like?"

I blushed. "Fair enough. From the little I know, I have learned that he has a high sense of Confucian morality but a certain rigidity of thought. We have talked about our feelings and our beliefs. He is a keen observer, yet he isn't imaginative except in military strategy. His men are quite loyal to him. He rarely takes the time to think deeply about life. He wants always to act. It is as though he is moved by some constantly driving force. Those who know him say he is quick to anger and quick to seek revenge. As you have seen, he can be forgiving, but I have also heard that he can be very cruel to his enemies. I haven't seen that side of him; I find it hard to believe." I paused, "But I cannot imagine caring for any other."

"You have convinced me that I am in the right camp even though I came here under strange circumstances."

The days while I was recovering were lazy and pleasant, but I was losing weight and felt listless. When I looked into a mirror, I saw dark circles under my eyes and the lids looked a transparent blue. The scar on my face was healing well. It was still red now. I could only hope that when it turned white, just a thin line would remain.

"Feng," I said one morning, "the longer I am away from Wu, the more insecure I feel."

Feng looked at me and shook his head. He said, "But you told me that you wanted to be independent."

"Well, I don't feel independent now," I replied.

"I heard that Wu has captured the men who tortured you and is on his way back here." Feng said.

"Wonderful, we will go out to meet him"

Feng looked at me with doubt. "You don't seem well enough yet."

I replied sharply, "Let me be the judge of that. Just get things ready."

As soon as we were underway, I realized that it had been a mistake. I was feeling especially sick from the jolting and swaying of the sedan chair. "Well this is what you get for being so headstrong," I thought. I was pinning my hopes on magic…the sight of Wu's face.

We had not traveled far when Feng shouted, "There is the general."

I saw Wu galloping towards us with a group of his men behind him.

"Now I will feel better," I told myself.

Wu jumped from his horse and ran to my sedan chair. "Rare timing," he shouted. His face was suffused with excitement, yet I felt that it wasn't because of me alone.

"Hurry, Bourtai. You have come at just the right moment."

Reining in his horse he lifted me up behind him. We galloped to a circle of men. There he leapt down and pulled me down roughly. He held my hand and dragged me into the circle where I came face to face with Ma. Even though Ma was tied to a small tree, I shrank back involuntarily.

"You will never again need to fear this man," Wu said to me in triumph, "I will have my revenge for all the wounds he and Li's army have inflicted. He will regret making you suffer so."

I did not like this Wu who was standing beside me. His gloating face was as inhuman as a Peking Opera mask. At that moment, I feared him almost as much as I had feared Ma.

Ma was certain that he was going to die. He became defiant. "Should I live," he spat out, "I'm sure I would find many more beautiful than she." He looked directly at me.

Wu recoiled as from a physical blow. He moved to Ma deliberately so that he was standing directly over him. He placed his hands on either side of Ma's head forcing it upward. Ma was compelled to look directly into Wu's eyes. I saw Wu's shoulders convulse in one strong movement as he pressed his thumbs down into Ma's eyes. An inhuman scream came from Ma. Blood spattered everywhere. Wu's hands dripped a sickening red. With a negligent movement, as though he was shaking water from his hands, Wu shook the blood onto the ground, wiped his hands on the grass and then unsheathed his sword. He hacked Ma's arms above the ropes which bound him to the pole. Ma fell forward, arms outspread. His hands lay behind the tree.

"Hold his arms up so that he doesn't bleed to death and call the physician," Wu shouted to several of his men, "I have changed my mind. He does not deserve an easy escape from this life. Care for him and feed him until his arms have healed. Then we will turn him loose to see how he fares."

I closed my eyes, but the sun beat through my lids. I saw red everywhere. Stumbling through the crowd of jostling men I fell to the ground retching. Feng was holding back behind the perimeter of the crowd. He ran forward, picked me up, and carried me back to the sedan chair. The noise continued. After some time, I heard Feng talking to Wu in a soft voice.

"The journey has been too much for her. She is still very weak. I think she is asleep. I'll see that she is returned to camp."

"Let her sleep, then. I won't disturb her now," Wu said.

I leaned back and looked at the patterns of light on the curtains of my chair. My world had suddenly scattered into red shards around me. I truly knew Wu now, both his goodness and his evil. My despair was a sour knot in my stomach. Wu didn't come to see me that night. I could hear him carousing with his men. It made me sad to realize that, for the first time since I had known him, I preferred not to see him. I couldn't sleep with the horrible images that swam in my head. Now, if ever, I needed a mother to talk to.

Shortly after dark, I heard Wu's curses coming from his tent. Intermittently, Long Qiong, his Manchu lieutenant, gave low, measured responses to Wu's outburst, but I couldn't make out anything they were saying. I wondered vaguely what was happening; however, I was too absorbed in my own misery to care.

Toward the middle of the night, I was still staring into the darkness when I heard Long Qiong in the entrance to my tent.

"My lady, are you awake?" he asked.

I sat up quickly. "What is it?" The night was now still.

"Please come with me and talk to General Wu."

I entered Wu's tent. He was seated at his table with his head in his hands and his shoulders slumped over. This was another side of Wu that I had never seen before.

"I'm an idiot," he said bitterly, "My thirst for revenge has put us in a terrible position. Instead of delaying on our way to Peking to take revenge on Ma and his men, I should have marched my army to the city without rest. A runner has reported that Li Zhicheng is in the Forbidden City now and has declared himself emperor."

Long Qiong spoke. "Then we must leave with your army at once. Your troops and Dorgon's can surely overcome an undisciplined army like Li's. Dorgon has heard about Li's pillaging and his brutal treatment of the citizens of Peking. Dorgan sent a proclamation ahead granting amnesty and reinstatement to any officials, civil servants or common people who will surrender and declare fealty to you and Dorgon. He thinks it is wise to start the Qing reign with as much peace and new prosperity as possible."

"Qing reign!" Wu was livid. "That was not my bargain with Dorgon. He said he would help me restore the Ming Dynasty!"

Long looked frightened but he continued. "General, you are not now in any position to argue with Dorgon."

Wu looked sick. "You are right. I must do what is most prudent. At least I will have Bourtai with me."

He swiveled around and encircled my waist. I pulled away. I was not feeling well and wasn't even sure I wanted to be with him.

Li and his men fled Peking as Wu and Dorgon approached. Dorgon set about establishing the new Qing Dynasty. He used many of the old Ming civil servants and much of the mechanism of the previous rule; he was very benevolent with those who quickly declared fealty to the Qing. Wu needed something to occupy him. Along with other generals he readily accepted the task of defeating the remnants of Li's army and securing the capture of Li. Li managed to elude his pursuers; however, he was said to have met his death at the hands of some villagers from whom he was stealing supplies and food.

It was several months before Wu returned. I dreaded seeing him because I knew I was pregnant and it was obvious. He had a puzzled expression when he saw me.

"Wu," I said, "I am going to have a child. It might be yours, but it could be from the rape."

I expected a roar of anger; instead, he put his arms around his shoulders and just rocked himself back and forth with tears streaming down his face. Finally, he straightened. He looked directly at me and said, "You will have to kill it. We can't be sure. We will have many sons later. Surely you know someone who can help you. Often dead children are found lying by the sides of the roads or are dropped into lakes. Women know how to do these things."

I was shocked, although I shouldn't have been after what I had seen him do earlier, but hearing him say such a thing tore at my heart.

"Wu, I can not do that. This child is part of me too. Killing it is something I just can't do."

He looked at me as though I had lost my senses. "But the father, he could be anyone. How could you want such a child?"

I just stood there helpless to explain my feelings. "I don't know. I really don't know. Please just let me go away and give birth. I will leave the child somewhere."

He seemed overwhelmed. He shook his head in disbelief. "Bourtai I can't deny you this even though the thought of another man's child fills me with rage. This was not your fault. Go then, but remember this oath; if I ever see this child or know where it is, I will kill it myself. Hide it well. I don't want to know anything about it."

I was shaking. It had taken all my courage to confront him. I turned and ran. But he was going to let me and the child live. I needed to plan where I could go before he changed his mind. It would be difficult, but I couldn't destroy this life in my body. I tried to work out a plan with Feng's help. "We could go to Shenyang where Mamu lives," I suggested. I was certain she would welcome us.

"We can travel as Buddhist pilgrims," Feng said.

"But Buddhist pilgrims would not have horses," I replied.

"You're right." He thought a minute. "Perhaps I could be your brother protecting you on your way. Our family could have provided the horses. You should stay back when we are near a village. I'll buy provisions."

We talked more, but we couldn't come up with a better solution.

"We'll have to try our luck with this plan," I said. "Are you sure you want to go with me?"

"I can never make up for what I did to you when you were Ma's captive. I will always go with you wherever you decide to go."

We made pilgrims' robes from coarse cloth and attached hoods that would hide our faces. We were working to devise a poor peasant's garb when Long Qiong, Wu's lieutenant, came to the tent. He brought us a heavy purse with silver taels along with smaller coins.

"Wrap them separately so that they don't jingle, and sew them to your undergarments. Here are some hundred-year old eggs and some cucumbers for liquid. I will provide you with the strongest horses we have. General Wu said he will watch for your return."

This astonished me. I hadn't thought of the possibility of Wu in my life again. I knew I was still very attracted to him, but could I accept him as he was? And could he be with me again without thinking of what had happened to me? It seemed that too much divided us.

Feng and I left in the morning while it was still dark. I knew Wu would hear us leaving, but he remained in his tent. It was possible I would not see him again.

CHAPTER 6

Feng and I traveled mostly by night when the moon was bright enough to light our way. We avoided the main roads and hid in the forests or up a mountainside away from the road in order to avoid the bandits who roamed everywhere. We often slept during the day. Many times we could find a monastery to shelter in. Usually, the monks would feed us and also give us cold cooked rice and a few vegetables to carry with us. When we couldn't find a monastery, Feng would go alone to a village in the early evening to buy food for us and grain for the horses. As we traveled we learned about each other's lives. I knew Feng had come from a peasant family, so I was curious about how he had learned calligraphy. He recounted his early life with his farming family. Their land was poor. His family owned too little land to provide for him, his parents and his two older brothers. The only salvation for his family had seemed to be to sell him to become a palace eunuch.

"I was very young when I became a eunuch. Fortunately, I was assigned to an older eunuch who was in charge of the kitchen supplies. He wanted me to learn sums and how to write simple orders, so he began to teach me calligraphy. I knew much by the time that Peking was overthrown. Then, I was captured by some of Li's soldiers."

Here he paused and stared into space in recollection. I remembered Feng telling me that he had also been badly used by the soldiers. I knew his memories must be as painful as mine were. Would these memories stay with us always?

I wanted to distract him, so I said, "But tell me more about the calligraphy. What did you learn?"

"Oh yes, the calligraphy—I am so sorry for what I wrote."

"I know what Ma whispered in my ear," I replied, "But I haven't looked at my belly. I rub it with ointment to heal the scars, but, even so, I can't bear to see it."

"I didn't know how to write what Ma told me," Feng said, "so I wrote the first things I could think of which was 'Wu's lady'. I hoped none of Ma's soldiers would read it, and they didn't."

My torture had been so awful when it was happening. Wu's lady indeed! But now, I began to laugh until tears were streaming down my face and my scars ached. Sometimes life was so absurd! Feng was suddenly embarrassed by the forced intimacy we were sharing. He changed the subject quickly.

"What will we do when we get to Shenyang?" he asked.

"We can both stay with my grandmother, but the fewer people who know we are there, the better. Word of my whereabouts cannot get back to Wu."

"But how can we get into the palace looking like this?"

"Long Qiong gave me a letter to permit us to pass through the gate at Shan Hai Guan, but getting into the palace could be a problem. When we get near to Shenyang, we should be able to find a river to bathe in. Then you can approach the sentries and tell them you have a message for Master Yang which is very important. Say that you must deliver it personally. I will write something that you can show the guards. The guards will probably not be able to understand *putonghua*. I will write the note in Manchu, but you will have to learn a few phrases of Manchu to explain what you want. I am sure Master Yang will think of some way to get us past the sentries. Tell Master Yang to wait until after dark to fetch me. Few people will notice us then. I'll wait some distance away until you come for me. If you have any problems, there are Chinese merchants in the city who would probably help you."

When we slept during the day, we unbridled the horses and removed the saddles. We let them roam so that they would seem to be wild horses or lost horses if someone came across them. A sharp whistle always brought them trotting back to us.

One night, a torrential rain beat down incessantly. We weren't near a monastery or a village. There was no hope of traveling on without losing our way. Feng cut pine boughs, and shook them off as well as he could. We spread them under an outcropping of rocks and spread more over us for cover. As we huddled together for warmth, I was glad for someone who was more than a servant. He had become a true friend.

The next morning was bright with the sun. We found a small pond hidden far from view of the road and decided to bathe and lay our clothes out into the sun to dry. I bathed first in my shift while Feng stood watch for anyone coming by. Then it was my turn to stand watch. Feng stripped and jumped into the water like a little boy. His lithe body seemed so vulnerable. I began to cry because of what had been done to him. He would never have the pleasures most of us enjoy.

When we came to a monastery, Feng stayed silent. I told the monks that he was my mute brother and that we were heading to the coast to find a boat to take us to Putuo Shan, an island in the Bo Hai Gulf. Generally we got the same response. The monks told us that we were not traveling at the right season.

They said, "Most pilgrims visit the island in April on Kuan Yin's birthday. It is most auspicious then. That's when she works her miracles."

"Yes," I would say. "We know that, but we couldn't leave sooner. We had to wait until my elder brother returned to take care of our ailing parents."

"Ah," the monks would respond. "Surely your filial piety will go a long way toward making a miracle occur."

"We can only hope so," I replied. They nodded mutely.

"Do you believe in miracles?" Feng asked me later.

"I'm not sure. I'd like to."

"When I die, I will never be a whole man. All eunuchs want to be buried with their private parts. In that way they are assured of becoming a man again in the afterlife. Most eunuchs keep their personal parts in a small box which they guard with great care. When I was captured by Li Zhicheng's men, I wasn't able to take my box with me." He looked cruelly distressed.

I turned him to face me. "Feng," I said, "if there are acts on earth that derive merits in heaven, then surely you will have a miracle and be whole again." He seemed comforted.

When we reached Shan Hai Guan, we were given everything we needed and were urged to rest there before continuing our journey. The hardest stretch was still ahead of us, but at least I was in my home land.

CHAPTER 7

The trip from Shan Hai Guan to Shenyang seemed almost as long as the trip from Peking to Shan Hai Guan, but the weather was warm and the commander at the Shan Hai Guan pass gave us an armed escort and provisions to last for a number of days. I was getting over my nausea, but the jolting of the horse tired me. My back ached constantly. If we walked with our horses over rough terrain, then my feet became blistered and bloody. Feng was like a mother hen with me. He insisted that we stop frequently, and when we came to a stream, he often bathed my feet. The soldiers from the escort didn't quite know what to make of us. I heard one of them say, "Why has this ragged pair been given so much attention, and why would the man bathe a woman's feet?"

I knew that Long Qiong must have worded his instructions wisely so as to hide our identities. He well knew of Wu's threat concerning the child I was carrying.

When we reached the point where we could see Shenyang in the distance, I said to the soldiers, "Your help has been most welcome. My brother and I will rest here before entering the city. There is no need for you to remain with us now that we have arrived safely. And please return the horses your commander loaned to us. We no longer need them."

This caused a little consternation and much discussion among the soldiers. Their mission had been to see us safely to Shenyang. Could they leave us just short of the city? Finally, the leader decided that the mission, whatever its nature, had been accomplished and that they could turn back. Feng and I rested on a knoll near the city eating a small amount of cold rice and hundred-year eggs which I was beginning to dislike very much.

When the sun began to set, I rehearsed Feng again in his Manchu speech. He was reluctant to leave me. I urged him on. "You must go now. We don't want to spend the night outside the safety of the city. We're so close! I'll stay hidden. I'm certain you will succeed. Be firm with the sentry and insist on seeing Master Yang in person."

Feng straightened his back and took off rapidly. I was not as confident as I pretended, but I knew if he could reach Master Yang, everything could be worked out. The hours seemed like days; the damp of the night settled in, and every strange sound made me start. Only the chirp of the crickets was reassuring. Finally, I saw several figures coming toward me with a lantern. I had never been so happy to see the faces of Feng and Master Yang as I was at that moment.

Master Yang bowed to me in a very formal way. "I see you have returned as a lady of some note," he said.

I laughed. "No, I am the same difficult student you have always known – just a little older and much more exhausted –bigger too." I patted my belly. "I don't want it known that I am pregnant. I want to stay hidden until after the baby is born."

"We will be closer to your grandmother's compound in the palace by going to the west gate. I'm sorry to have to put out the light as we get closer, but in the dark, no one will know who we are," Yang said.

It was obvious that Feng had explained the problem to him as they came to get me. What would Mamu think when she saw me and my condition? I was so certain of her love that I knew that I would be welcomed in any condition. And so I was. We decided that Master Yang should go to Mamu's gate and ask to speak to her personally. Feng and I had smeared dirt on our faces and I pulled my hood over my head so that it would hide as much of my face as possible. The servants were reluctant to call Mamu to the gate, but Yang convinced them that it was most urgent. Someone had been hurt. Feng and I stayed back.

When Mamu came to the gate, Master Yang said, "Madam I am asking your help for two Buddhist pilgrims who were set upon by bandits outside the city. One of them is injured and needs a place to rest. He also has a young companion with him. I will vouch for them both if you will give them shelter."

Mamu was known for her generosity and her piety, so no one would be surprised that she would take us in. We were whisked through the courtyard to a bed chamber with a small garden behind. She gasped when I threw back my hood and spoke to her in a whisper. "Shh, it must be a secret that we are here. Please send the servants to bed so that we can talk. I'm not really injured, but that was the best pretext we could think of for getting into your compound."

I had much to tell her and Master Yang. I explained what had taken place. When Mamu heard of the rape she began to wail.

"Hush," I admonished her, "it is over now. We can't risk having others know who we are. I don't want our presence here known. It might get back to Wu."

We huddled in the garden and made plans. I was very fortunate. Girten, the servant I had known when I was a child, was still with Mamu. Girten was about as far along in carrying a child as I was. We decided that the cook and the other two servants should be sent to the house of Mamu's friend on the other side of Shenyang. The friend's granddaughter, who was living there, had just given birth to twins and the household was in turmoil. Mamu's servants would be a great help to them.

Feng said, "If it is all right with you and Master Yang, we can stay here with you and do the work of the servants. Also, if she is trustworthy, keep the woman who is expecting the child here. We can swear her to secrecy. When she and Bourtai have their children, we can say that they are her twins."

Master Yang shook his head grinning, "It is a strange plan, but I am in agreement. It could just succeed. And the company will be most pleasant if we are not worked too hard." He gave Mamu a meaningful look. She just humphed in return.

I was lucky to have many of the silver taels left that Long Qiong had given us. Mamu called her servant, Girten, in. I explained that I couldn't raise the baby I was pregnant with as my own. I asked her if she would raise it along with her own child. After some thought, she agreed. When she saw the silver I was giving her, she said she wouldn't take it, but I finally persuaded her that she could use it for the babies.

"You must remember," Mamu said. "No one must know."

When Girten left, Mamu said, "I can assure you Girten will keep your secret. She doesn't need a bribe to be loyal, but it will certainly be welcome to her in her circumstances. She hasn't told me who the father of her baby is, but I imagine he is long gone from here."

Thus, we all settled in for a long wait. The summer was unusually hot and I became more and more uncomfortable. Master Yang and Feng managed Mamu's household well. They even found time for Feng and me to study more. Of course, like most women, Mamu believed that eggs were an essential part of a pregnant woman's diet. She even bought two laying hens. She said, "Feng, you will be in charge of these. Make sure we have plenty of eggs for our two women."

Feng gave her a puzzled look. Just how was he to persuade the hens to lay eggs?

Some evenings we played a chess game. I was experiencing a calm interlude in my life, but it was too calm and I fretted over the future. Once in a while I would sigh and say to Feng, "I wish I could hear more news from China."

Of course, Feng knew exactly what I meant. I missed Wu terribly, but had to wrestle with whether I would return to him or not. I did not want to leave my child with Mamu even though I knew the baby would have excellent care, but there was nothing for me here. My life seemed to be tied to that of Wu's.

One day Mamu took my hand and led me to the garden. "Bourtai, you and your child are welcome here as long as you like, but I'm afraid you will not have a very satisfying life if you stay here. Feng has told me that you can return to your general. That is truly amazing. Most men would be different. I can tell you want to be with him. That chance is not something to be tossed away lightly. Most women never have that option. Girten will be able to nurse both children. I would love to have a child in the house again. Think about it. We can talk more, later."

That is all I did think about. My mind was constantly going in circles. I couldn't sleep, not only because I was getting bigger and more uncomfortable, but also because of the decision I had to make. Wu was the center of my life. I had witnessed an almost unimaginable dark side to him that I could never forget. I knew I would be sure to see that side of him again if I returned, but I had seen a better side too. I don't know what I expected of him. His job, his life, was to fight and to kill. Many times he must have had to look at his own men lying on the ground like butchered animals. He must wonder if there was any meaning to it all. I also knew that when I looked at the child I was carrying, I would see not only a reflection of myself, but also a reminder of a horror I carried with me no matter whose child it was. I talked more with Mamu.

"If you decide to leave the child with me, don't become too attached to it. Think of it as Girten's. Leave its care to us. Your mother had to leave you, yet you were a happy child with many advantages. I loved you with all my heart. I will make sure that this child will be well taken care of and loved just as much as you were and are."

I cried. "If only I knew. I can't be certain who the child's father is."

She just held me and rocked me in her arms.

The fall and then the winter months came all too swiftly. Master Yang spent time instructing Feng in all manner of things. To everyone's surprise, Feng turned into an excellent cook. Our constant praise made him beam. Sometimes he even made eggs palatable; nevertheless, I kept eyeing the chickens with dislike.

I fumed, "I can't wait to wring their necks so that you can present us with a fine chicken stew and we can forget the eggs."

Girten was a very quiet woman, but as we talked more, I learned that her background had been hard. She was the last daughter of a peasant family who had too many girls and too little land. She had been given away at an early age as a servant. Many peasant girls were. Her story was much like Feng's.

She sighed as she talked about her younger years. She said, "I suppose I was lucky really. So many unwanted daughters are drowned or found strangled at birth and lying in a ditch. At least my parents found me a home. Your grandmother has been good to me, but I keep thinking about my family. I can't even remember what my mother and father look like."

I couldn't bring myself to tell her all of what had happened to me, but she sensed that I had not had a completely easy life either after I left Shenyang. Our feelings and our pregnancies united us in a certain way. I was pleased to find that I still genuinely liked her and would trust her with my child. It made my decision easier. Despite my fears, I would try to go back to Wu.

CHAPTER 8

The cold began early that year. By the end of October the ground was massed with snow. We closed the shutters over the lattice windows, and built fires. The rooms of our compound opened onto a large walled courtyard. Occasionally, on sunny days we could open doors or windows into the courtyard and enjoy the sunlight if it wasn't too cold. At least the walls around the city kept the wind at bay, but the days were dark and seemed incredibly long. My heart was gray and my spirit cold. Our ample bedchamber had a large *kong* in it on which several people could sleep very comfortably. The *kong* was a platform of brick with a hollow area inside through which a pipe from our cooking stove pushed warm air. We piled quilts and furs on top of the *kong* and remained quite warm at night. Feng and Master Yang slept next to it on the floor curled up in quilts and more furs. We sat on the *kong* to eat our meals, do embroidery, work at lessons or just talk.

Girten and I began to feel our babies' movements in the same week. We often tried to image what little body part was making a lump in the side or front of our bellies. Sometimes a kick would send a piece of bread flying that we had balanced on our stomachs. Then everyone laughed. Girten spent a lot of time worrying over a name for either a boy or a girl, but I was reluctant to try to name a child which I might leave. I was beginning to feel like a hibernating bear; nevertheless, I still had to eat; bears didn't. And Feng was becoming quite the cook.

Girten often left the palace for a short walk, but I made do with circling around the courtyard because I didn't want anyone from outside to know I was there. One particularly snowy day Girten went out, but returned almost immediately. I went to open the gate. She was grimacing and moving very slowly.

"Girten, has it started?"

"Yes, I don't feel very good. Can you help me to the *kong*?" She walked a few steps, then stopped and made little yelping noises like a wounded puppy.

"Hurry," I said, "you must lie down. I'll get the others."

Neither of us knew what to expect. We were both frightened. We would have to rely on the help of Mamu and the help of the men who probably had no more idea what to do than I did.

Mamu became the general. "Feng, boil plenty of water. Master Yang, please find the clean cloths I have cut into strips. They're in a bag on the back shelf near the furs. Bourtai, sit here and hold Girten's hand. It always helps if you can squeeze someone's hand."

Girten lay there for what seemed hours gulping air in then emitting sharp cries.

Mamu began to look worried. She leaned over and whispered in my ear, "The baby doesn't seem to be coming. We're going to have to do something soon. She can't go on like this." Then she said, "Girten—"Girten push—push."

"I am. I am. Oh, I can't stand it." She began to scream, "Oh, get it out of me. Please, please. Help me!" She was crying.

"The head should be coming down, but I don't see it," Mamu said. Then we both saw the problem. The baby was trying to come out backwards. Girten was being torn. Her screams terrified me. I had never imagined birth could be so bad. Mamu yelled at Feng. "Get me some tongs. We've got to pull the baby out."

Girten gave several more screams and then lost consciousness. Mamu grabbed what looked like a leg and pulled. There was a rush of blood and the baby popped out with the cord wrapped around its neck. As we hurried to untangle it, I could see that it looked awful. Mamu held it by its feet and smacked it several times. It didn't breathe. It just hung there limp and blue. Mamu slid down to the floor with the baby in her lap and began to weep. She rocked herself and the baby back and forth. "I tried," she whispered, "I tried."

A few minutes before, the room was filled with noise. Now even Feng and Master Yang sat quiet and immobile. We all seemed paralyzed. Finally Feng roused himself and walked over. "Give the baby to me. I'll take it away." None of us asked where.

Mamu seemed to come out of her shock. "We need to stop the bleeding. We can use the strips of cloth to pack her and hope that will help."

Girten was still unconscious. We packed her, then we wrapped her in furs and I slid beside her on the *kong* and held her while ghostly images swirled around in my head. Even when we thought death was far away, it could be very close.

Feng returned after about an hour. He was cold and shaking. I got him some tea and threw a quilt over his shoulders.

I started to ask, "Feng, where…"

He just held up his hand and shook his head. "No dogs will find the baby." But then tears began to stream down his face and his shaking became worse.

"We need to sleep," I said. "Come, lie near the *kong*. It will warm you." I moved back onto the kong between Mamu and Girten. I put my arm around Girten. Although she slept, she moaned constantly. I wedged a part of the quilt between us so that she would not feel my baby kicking. All of us had a fitful night. Even Master Yang did not maintain his calm but snored in spurts and startled awake several times, and Feng called out in his sleep with little cries.

With morning, Girten did not seem to know what had happened. Mamu had to tell her again and again that her baby had died. Girten sobbed most of the day as we moved around her like shadows, afraid to disturb her more. Finally Mamu said, "We must get her to pump her milk to keep it flowing until your baby is born. I know it seems cruel, but there is no other course."

"Oh Mamu," I wailed, "Everything is so awful and I'm frightened. We can't ask her to do that."

She took me in her arms and stroked my back. "If you are going to leave here, Girten will have to nurse your baby. If you start nursing, you won't be able to leave it. Hush now," she said. "Last night *was* awful, but most births aren't so difficult. We need to comfort Girten now. Her pains must be dreadful."

I knew she meant the pains of Girten's heart as well as her body. Mamu went to Girten and spoke to her softly, but Girten kept sobbing.

"My baby was all I had left of the man I loved. Now that is gone too," Girten said.

None of us knew who that man was, but I thought of Wu and wished with all my heart that the baby I carried was his. It was my child, but it might also be the child of one of my torturers. I both loved and hated the baby I was carrying. Perhaps it was best that I would be leaving it, and Girten would have a child to hold and love more than I ever could.

I tried to comfort Girten, but as the time approached for my own baby's birth, I became more depressed and fearful. I knew the birth would be very soon. Could I possibly be as brave as Giriten had been?

The snow was covering everything in heavy sheets of white and the wind insinuated itself into every corner. As night approached, things became only black or white shapes. Nothing seemed real. The only color and light came from our fire which made our shadows loom large against the walls like angry demons.

A stirring in the courtyard outside awoke us. The snow-muffled sound of many horses' hooves moved near our compound. We listened intently. It was a strange time of night for a group to be entering the palace grounds in the midst of a storm.

Shortly after we heard the sounds from outside, someone rapped on the door. Mamu and Feng sprang up with a start and ran to the door. Mamu gasped and then began to sob.

"I can't believe it," she cried, "I can't believe it is you. How is it that you are here?"

I stared at the woman who stood in the doorway. It was like looking at myself as I might be in twenty some years.

"Mama," the woman said, "My husband was summoned here by Dorgon. I begged to come with him to see you."

Mamu shouted, "Bourtai, come. It's your mother."

The night was so strange that I felt I might be imagining this happening. I ran and then stopped a few feet in front of this stranger. I suddenly felt constrained. I did not know this woman. Could she really be my mother, the woman I had dreamed about most of my life? She ran forward and clasped me tightly in her arms.

"Bourtai, oh, you are a woman now. I have missed so much of your life. Neither of us will ever get it back, but we are here together now, even for a short time, and it is a miracle. Let me look at you. You have become a beautiful woman."

I thought my heart would crack. I tried to say Mama, but couldn't, only sobs came out. We held each other for a long time before Mamu gently led us to the table and poured tea for everyone. My mother's words and mine came rushing out in torrents. We tried to tell each other about years of our lives, but the telling could only be outlines of years.

Mamu interrupted us. "How long can you stay? How is it that you are here?"

My mother took my hand as she explained. "Mamu must have told you that shortly after my husband was killed, I was bartered to the chieftain of one of our enemy tribes. I was the cement to hold my new husband's people and our people together. My husband is not unkind to me. But he didn't want the girl child of another man. This is the way it is with men. There was nothing I could do. I beg you to try to understand, Bourtai. I knew Mamu would take care of you as well as anyone could. I was able to bear my new husband a son which has given him much honor, so he is well pleased with me and granted my wish to see my mother. I hoped you would be here, but it has been so long I was afraid you might be gone."

Mamu beamed. "Well, now you are just in time to help your daughter with her baby. Pray that it comes soon."

Our prayers were answered. The next morning my water broke and the pains started. It was the most pain I had ever felt, in some ways even worse than my torture had been, but in other ways not as bad because I knew I was giving a new life to the world. Having my mother and grandmother there beside me encouraged me to be brave. Five hours after the pains started, an angry, squirming child lay on my belly. She was wet and shiny like a seal and waved her little feet and fists in the air as though incensed to have to come out into the light from the nice warm place where she had been. Even Girten roused from her misery and came over to exclaim and smile at the new arrival. Mamu cleaned the baby off and then placed her in Girten's arms. "Now she is yours. You will be in charge of her. She may be hungry already."

Girten looked at her tentatively at first; then she grasped the baby more tightly and gave a shy smile. "I'll be very good to her. I'll have lots of milk. She will never have to fuss. Is it all right if she has a Chinese name? My baby's father was a Chinese soldier."

My mother was bewildered. "Why is your servant taking her?"

I felt strange, but I said, "Girten will be her mother."

I turned to Girten. "It is only right for you to name her. What will you call her?"

"Mei Hua," she said. "Beautiful Flower. It is a Chinese name."

Feng hovered over Girten and then shyly grasped the baby's tiny hand. From that moment on he was smitten. My mother leaned over the baby making soft sounds and sighing. "I am a grandmother now. This is payment for my tears. Life has turned once again. Girten, let me hold her for a while."

I feigned indifference. My mother stared at me in puzzlement. I met her eyes knowing that I would soon have to explain the situation and what had happened to me.

My mother turned to Mamu, "And you, Mama, are now a great-grandmother. We should all live so long."

My mother was able to stay for two more nights before her husband summoned her to return to their home. I told her about the rape and my reasons for not keeping the baby. She was tender with me and said, "Women do not fare well in life. I understand. Happiness is often short and sorrow can be long."

After she left, I realized that I hadn't even asked her what her husband's name was—what he was like—and even worse on my part, hadn't asked anything about my step-brother. My shame was devastating to me. I had thought only of myself. Now, I would have to hope to see my mother again some time in the future and know more about her life.

I tried to ignore my baby, but when no one was looking, I stared at her trying to find a likeness to Wu. It was futile. She didn't even look much like me.

CHAPTER 9

The winter days dragged on. Although I was in Shenyang, my mind was elsewhere with Wu. He was not the man I wished he were, but I still could not help wanting to be with him.

Mamu bound my breasts so that the milk which was coming in would dry up, but, at first, every time the baby cried, my breasts became engorged. Girten had named my child Mei Hua (Beautiful Flower). She truly was. Her eyes were dark and quick even before she was able to focus well, and her skin was soft as velvet. I tried to remain detached from her. I knew in my heart that if I stayed to raise her, every time she did something I didn't like, I would think of the rapists rather than thinking her actions were just those of a child. She couldn't go with me back to Wu because of his threat to kill her. I had to be honest with myself. I wanted the life I could have with Wu more than I wanted this child.

When I saw Feng, Girten and the others constantly buzzing around her, I felt envy and enormous guilt. I began to slip out of the compound at night, especially in heavy snow when I could be anonymous. I savored the beauty and silence of the *hutongs* (small alleys) near where we lived. These walks restored my balance; I practiced the meditation that Master Wang had taught me long ago. Only after these walks, when I slipped through the door late at night, could I fall into a sleep without dreams. Other nights, though, I dreamed of empty blood-red eye sockets and woke trembling.

When I was awake, I could guard myself by monitoring my thoughts. I remembered how Wu had lightly stroked my face pausing for a second at the small scar at the side of my mouth. I was very self-conscious about it, but he would say, "It merely makes you more mysterious and intriguing."

Then he would move his hand down to the hollow in my throat where he could feel the beat of my heart. His hand touching lightly there was intensely arousing. After a pause, he would begin an inventory of my body, still with the same slow deliberate movements and the softest touch. By the time he was between my legs, I would have gone crazy with desire. My memories of this were what I lived for. When I was alone at night, I would touch all the places he had touched. I would drift off into a world of sensual dreams. I could picture his hands, strong and large with the jade thumb ring he wore to help him draw the strings of his bow. I could recall his eyes, black as his hair. When he was facing battle they were like pieces of obsidian, but when he was with me, his eyes were lustrous, changing with his moods.

At times I wondered if he was the same with other women as he was with me. I knew there *were* others – certainly Chen Yuan Yuan, his celebrated concubine, his wife, and the women he used who were near his battles. I attempted to crush these thoughts, but women knew that this had always been the way of Chinese men. Women were theirs to enjoy. I was determined to compete well; I could be more inventive than other women, and I had learned a skill that few Chinese women knew, dancing.

When it was warm enough, I spent time in the back garden practicing the dances I had been taught by the exotic foreigners. I thought I was being secretive, but I soon found out that Feng and Girten could not contain their curiosity. They spied on my practice. I did exactly what the foreign women I had watched did. I danced toward where they were hiding and grabbed their hands pulling them into the garden. After that, I had an audience.

One day Feng said, "I am not a whole man, but my eyes and heart are those of a man. I thank you for giving me the dances. They will be treasures in my mind."

57

It was such a truly personal thing Feng said to me that it broke my heart. Eunuchs and women had a common bond. Men were the masters!

Girten became very interested in helping me fashion new dance costumes. I had the one I had been given; she knew what it looked like. She began to giggle. She said, "I'm sure I can find you the materials you will need in the market place. Together we can make another one."

Actually, we sewed two, one for me and one for Girten. She pretended that she didn't want it.

She said, "I will never have a use for this."

But I could tell that she was pleased.

I replied, "You never know what life will bring. You may be able to use it some time."

We both had a costume that any man would find alluring. They were even more attractive than the original. A wide gold belt fitted low on our hips. Then we attached sheer silk to the inside of the belt. The skirt billowed like a cloud when we turned. For the top we used red silk with sparkling beads on it—just enough to cover our breasts. Somewhere Girten had even found tiny bells which we laced onto ties around our ankles. I encouraged Girten to try her costume on. She was reluctant at first, but then she shyly donned it, blushing. She held her hands in front of her face, twirling like a little girl.

At times I wished things would stay the way they were. The few of us who were there together made a comfortable group.

Feng and Master Yang took turns as cook. At times, Master Yang did not behave as strictly celibate as most Buddhist monks professed to be. We could tell that he found Mamu attractive. She enjoyed his companionship also.

If he was cooking I would hear Mamu say, "Here, let me help you. You must be tired."

He would take a spoonful of soup from a pot and say, "Mamu, what does this need?" Their heads would come together in an intimate movement as she leaned in toward him.

"Maybe just a little more *lajiao*," she answered. After he added the peppers, then both of them would taste the dish and smile at each other.

"Perfect! It is perfect now, Master Yang. You are such a talented man."

He often gave a wide grin after her praise. Mamu taught him some of the northern dishes and how to cut meat for a hot pot into which everyone dipped meat on a stick. The pots were intricately made and were the pride of many households in the north. The boiling oil gave off a pungent smell and the cooking meat and vegetables whetted the appetite.

Feng was the more artistic cook. His dishes were presentations. Sliced carrots would be the antennae of a butterfly. Thin slices of potatoes would be cut into wing shapes with the center of the insect being a molded paste of meat. Eyes might be any vegetable, mushrooms, bracken or radishes. We were like children delighted by his concoctions and looked forward to each production.

Feng often fed Mei Hua. He crushed vegetables and then waved them through the air like a flying insect. She would giggle and open her mouth wider than we thought possible. This very diminutive woman had captured Feng. Sometimes, though, she used her womanly prerogative to clamp her mouth shut, and no cajoling could make her open it.

I read quite a bit, and embroidered, and painted. I had been lucky enough to make a quick sketch of my mother during the short time she was here. I would later make it into a painting to hang on my ancestor's wall. I worked on a quilt for Mei Hua. It was thick with batting and intricately embroidered on the front. I gave this to Girten. I even designed a pattern for leather dress boots of the finest leather. Feng took the pattern to a leather worker and asked him to make a pair of boots for me. The boots were to have rigid soles for riding horseback. I also asked Feng to get larger pieces of leather made with the same design. He was too polite to ask me why I wanted the larger pieces. When he returned with the finished boots and leather, I was more than pleased.

Despite all my time spent as a child with Master Yang when he was teaching me, I had not learned the skill of living in the moment. I thought constantly of returning to Wu and wondered what my reception would be.

The winter days turned into a soggy spring with mud everywhere and trees weeping with water. My impatience to travel grew. I knew, however, that traveling had to wait until the spring season turned into the lovely kind that I remembered from my childhood where the days were calm and sunny with a light breeze ruffling the trees.

The more impatient I grew, the sadder Feng seemed. He had grown so attached to Mei Hua that he acted as though she was his own child. He took me aside one day to plead his case. "When we leave here, you will want to know how Mamu and Mei Hua are doing. No matter where we are, I would like to make a short trip here each year so that I can reassure you that everyone is well."

I was touched by his need. Here was a family of his own devising for him to return to. These people had suddenly come to be of great importance to him.

I gave it some thought. "Well," I said. "That sounds like arduous journeys for you to make, but I would be grateful to have you do so."

He beamed with a smile like that of a little boy. I hoped that he would never lose that sense of joy.

CHAPTER 10

The cold rains which made me so impatient did their magic. One morning, as I looked through the lattice window, I saw green stretching everywhere. Buds perched in the trees like tiny birds. The whole world was transformed. This beauty meant one thing to me. Now I could travel.

I hurried to awaken Feng. He knew from the moment he saw my face that we would soon be leaving Shenyang. He tried to hide his own disappointment, but his response gave him away.

"Yes, I see. It is spring and we can travel. I will get ready for our journey." His voice was flat and his posture reluctant, but I was too excited to pay much attention. Long Qiong had sent a message saying that Wu had been assigned to the fortress at Jinzhou, and Wu wanted me to be with him. Was Long right? I had to believe so. The garrison at Jinzhou was not too far from Shenyang. I set about gathering my possessions. Long arranged an escort of Manchus to see me through the pass at Shan Hai Guan and on to Jinzhou.

When I finally arrived in Jinzhou, Wu came out to meet me. We stood looking at each other for a moment, then he gathered me in his arms and I knew I was where I wanted to be. For the night I was given a tent next to his. He promised me that we would take a short trip the next day. I was puzzled by this, but was so glad to be with him again that I didn't ask questions.

That night he appeared in the tent opening. I moved rapidly toward him. He reached out and ran his hands through my hair.

Lightening coursed through my body. Quickly, we made our way to the bedding and fell upon each other.

I shivered. Then I pressed myself into him. I heard his quick intake of breath. We made love as though we had never been apart. I disappeared into the sense of him, the smell of him, the movement and the urgency. I was soaring on a rising wind. We both made the high-pitched sounds of animals. Then with a cry, we exploded into the sky.

Afterwards, he rolled onto his back. I raised myself on my elbow to look at him. Yes, he was as I had dreamed of him all those nights---the same taut body and his chest, rising and inhaling slowly, was a muscular mound which dropped into a flat plain. I leaned over to kiss his nipple. He turned and lightly caressed my neck. All the resentment and longing I endured during that lonely winter disappeared.

"I'm beginning to know you well," he said. I began to sob. He held me tightly in his arms. Later he moved languidly as a cat and dressed himself. He left, but early the next morning he reappeared.

"Come, get dressed. I have a surprise for you."

We gathered our horses and rode out of the garrison into the countryside nearby. A lovely house stood on a knoll about a *li* away from the garrison. "How would you like to live there?" he asked.

"Isn't someone living there now?"

"Strangely enough it is empty. Would you like it? It is near the garrison and would be quite safe." I was mute. He led me into the house and I could see that it had never been occupied.

"Did you have it built for me?" I asked in disbelief.

"Now don't worry about such things. Do you like it? Do you want it?"

"Oh, yes, yes!" I ran through the doorway.

The main room was large. A *kong* wrapped around three sides. The kitchen stove would provide plenty of heat to keep the *kong* warm day and night.

Wu looked pleased with himself. "It is somewhat empty now but we can soon fix that. Some of your trunks will be at home here," he said wryly. "You will have to decide what you want. I will send men from the garrison to help you get settled. Tell them what you need and they will find it for you. Unfortunately, I have to get back to the garrison. I have many things to do."

He turned hesitantly. I thought he was about to say something else, but he just shook his head then immediately jumped on his horse and began galloping back to the garrison.

I ran into the house and lay on the bare *kong* and looked at the ceiling. This was for me? Could it really be mine? I stayed there in a sort of dream until I heard horses approaching. Men stood outside with my trunks and all manner of other things. There was more--- bedding, tables, chairs, pots and pans---just about anything I could need to run a household.

One of the men told me, "General Wu said that he would send some people to serve you. You can choose who you want. The people he chose will be here soon. If you find any unsuitable, you can send them away. They are local people who are happy to work for the general."

The men brought the things into the house. "Now, tell us where you want these put, then we will leave you alone," they said.

It seemed only a matter of hours before everything was in place in MY HOME. When the peasants came, I chose a house servant, a cook, a gardener and a man to look after the horses. He would also help with any other animals we might have. I enjoyed making the house mine. I even hung two of my paintings. When I explored the grounds, I found that the horses we had used to travel to the house were in a paddock near the back of the house. Wu must be planning to ride out with me as we used to do.

In front of my new home, a small pond glistened in the sun. A dock jutted out over the water. When I was settled, the gardener asked whether I would like to go fishing. I hadn't thought about fish in the pond, but the idea sounded interesting. We spent the next afternoon at the pond. I was thrilled to catch the fish. The only problem was that the gardener insisted that we return the fish to the water so that they could reproduce and keep the pond full. Occasionally he would pronounce one of the fish an *eating* fish.

It was for dinner. I always thought it was especially tasty if I had caught it.

I made short expeditions into the fields surrounding the house. Sometimes I went berry picking near the woods. Wu had warned me not to do that, but I always took my bow and arrows with me. I could track animals by their paw prints. I did see deer tracks, but never came across bear tracks. Once in a while I was able to shoot a rabbit. Rabbit stew made a fine addition to our meals. Bow hunting was something I did with my cousins when I was young. I was pleased to see that I hadn't lost my ability to shoot well.

It wasn't long after Wu's visits that I lost my appetite. Shortly after that, my monthly flow stopped. This was the first sign that I was pregnant. I was thrilled and couldn't wait to announce my condition to Wu.

"Wait," advised my servant girl, "sometimes babies don't stay."

I didn't see Wu for several months. By the time I did, I was obviously pregnant. Wu seemed to be almost as excited as I was when he saw me. He came up to me and patted my belly.

"A fine son?" he asked. "Correct?"

I nodded my head. I could only hope for a boy, but if I had a girl, I would love her with all my heart. I began to be ravenously hungry. Wu did everything an expectant father could. He no longer demanded sex and began to provide me with all kinds of delicacies. Before he left, he presented me with a box of foreign food called 'dates'. They were brown and looked very sticky, not appetizing at all, but to be polite, I took one from the box and bit off a small piece of the end. Soon I was popping two at a time into my mouth.

Wu stood there laughing. "I could tell by your face what you thought when you first saw these. You have changed your mind suddenly. Right?"

I licked my sticky fingers and smiled at him. "Thank you for my tasty gift."

He couldn't be with me much of the time, but couriers came with litchis. Bliss! I had never tasted anything as sublime as these round white orbs with just the right sweetness inside. Nuts, small oranges, and other delicious delicacies appeared; however, he didn't communicate with me for months. Still the time passed quickly. I began to worry. What if it is a girl? Girls don't count for much. I knew that many peasant women immediately killed girl babies, but I was no peasant woman. I raised my chin in defiance. She would be Wu's child and mine. That was all that mattered. The next time I saw him, he was full of news.

Smiling broadly he said, "The Emperor has made me a Prince of the Realm (One Who Pacified the West)."

I looked at him in astonishment. Then I jumped into his arms and he twirled me around.

"You seem to be heavier than I remembered," he said. "But my new honor is not too bad for our future is it?"

I just giggled and replied, "Yes, yes."

Then it occurred to me that I couldn't follow him everywhere he might be sent, especially with a child. Soon, I began to feel very heavy and ugly. Wu sensed this. One day before he returned to his garrison, he came up behind me and wrapped his arms around my growing belly. He held an exquisite mirror in front of my face. I stared at myself.

"You are one of the most beautiful women in the realm," he said. "This is my gift so that you will always remember that."

I dissolved into tears. Never had I seen such a remarkable gift. One side was smooth bronze so that I could see my reflection. The other side had herons flying across it among intricate clouds.

"How can I ever thank you? This is so precious to me."

"You will thank me when you have my son," he said.

After he was gone to his new post, I worried even more. What if the child *was* a girl?

Time went quickly. The months passed.

One day I had a bloody show. "The baby is coming," I told my servant. I thought I knew what to expect. After all, I had given birth before. When the pains began, I asked my servant to stay with me. The pains continued through the night and lasted all the next day.

My servant said, "We need to call a midwife now." She told the cook to go find a midwife quickly.

A short time later, a rather dirty, stocky peasant woman stood looking at me. "We must turn the baby around," she said.

I was horrified. Was I going to have the same trouble that Girten had? The pain seemed unbearable as she turned the baby.

"Ah now," the woman said in triumph. She pulled. "Now push, push."

It was a boy…a fat baby boy! I decided to call him Gaoxing. Wu would be so proud. I fell into a deep sleep. When I awoke, I felt a small warm pressure against my ribs and a soft tugging at my nipple. I smiled. "Not as strong yet as your father."

Once Wu had news of the birth, it was only days until he arrived to see his son. He came to the house with a contingent of men. As he swept Gaoxing up, he dropped the blankets around him and held him naked in the air for all his men to see. A shout of approval rose up. Wu could barely contain himself. He came inside. I looked up to see him holding our son and cooing. The servant laughed. Generals looked especially silly cooing.

"Well done," he said gently. He touched his finger to the tip of my nose and said, "I love you."

I was overcome by what he said. It was the first time he spoke of love. Then he added, "I am sorry that I have to leave you."

Even though Wu was gone, the few days that followed were the happiest days of my life.

CHAPTER 11

Wu San Gui was assigned to different military duties, but often his postings were very far away from Jinzhou. Skirmishes were necessary to rid the countryside of the remnants of the peasant army. He carried out his tasks diligently. Meanwhile, I remained in Jinzhou.

As I nursed Xiao (little) Gaoxing, the weeks went by. I missed Wu. Nevertheless, I was content in my own world with my baby. Gaoxing grew chubby. He chortled and giggled a lot, but very rarely cried. He sat up at three months. Then I began to notice something which caused me alarm. When he heard a sound, he immediately turned his head, but when a shadow or an object passed in front of him, he didn't react. Soon I was waving my hand back and forth in front of his face trying to get him to follow it. He didn't. Then I tried moving a bright red object back and forth, but he made no response. I was stunned. Maybe tomorrow he would react better. I settled both of us in for the night. He fell into a contented sleep, but I lay awake watching the shadows of whipping branches moving back and forth across the window with menace. The branches moved the way Gaoxing's eyes should have moved. Near dawn I fell into a bottomless dream. Images of Wu gouging out the eyes of Ma Xun haunted my sleep. I finally woke screaming. Xiao Gaoxing started to cry and several of the servants rushed in. I looked at them, a little dazed, still under the influence of the dream. Finally, I waved my hand at them in dismissal.

"It was nothing," I said. "Nothing."

But as the days went by, I became more convinced that the 'nothing' was something awful. Finally, I had to admit to myself that Gaoxing was blind. I shivered when I imagined how Wu would react. I only knew that my grief made my son even more precious to me. I would defend him and nurture him with all my strength.

At three months, although he could sit up by himself, he never reached for any object to play with. He always waited until it was handed to him. The cock crowing meant that it was morning. He would start to babble in his bed. The sound of pots and pans meant food. Even though he was still nursing, he began eating solid food after I had chewed it for him and then put it in his mouth. He could distinguish the sounds of different peoples' footsteps. He always brightened when Feng came into the room. He also knew the difference between day and night. When the house was quiet, it meant sleep. By ten months he began using words. He stood and began to walk but bumped into things and became quite frustrated. I removed all sharp-cornered objects that I could.

His attempts to walk made me weep. He wanted so much to explore the world, but it hit back at him at every turn. Feng spent hours helping him to walk and orienting him to every thing in the house.

In a few months, Wu returned between commissions. My voice shook as I told him that our son was blind. He was silent with his head down for what seemed to be an eternity. Then he turned and started to walk out of the room. "Well," he said, "I have other sons." And with that, he dismissed his son and mine.

Xiao Gaoxing became my life. I was determined to make his world the best that I could. Not only did he learn words quickly, but he also memorized stories and could tell them back to me word by word. He was proving to be very bright.

One morning, he woke up shouting, "Peixu hurt." I took him in my arms and told him that our cook, Peixu, was fine. But an hour later she spilled hot cooking oil all over her foot. The burn was so bad that she couldn't walk for a week. Similar things kept happening. Perhaps a gift had been given to him in exchange for his loss of sight. In any case, when he expressed a fear about doing something, we didn't do it.

Quite often it was the right choice. A cart we had intended to take to market overturned injuring all of its occupants. A runaway horse trampled a child on a road where he and Feng often walked. He knew ahead of time of bad things about to happen. He also knew when Wu would return. At these times, he became fretful. He would make himself as inconspicuous as possible. Wu persisted in ignoring him.

Gaoxing needed more than I could give him, so I sent to Shenyang to ask if Master Yang could join our household in order to educate Gaoxing. He agreed to come. Under his teaching, Gaoxing began to bloom.

He said, "I have two friends now, Feng and Master Yang."

Gaoxing began to grow rapidly. His curiosity was unbounded. As he felt his way around the house, he memorized every corner and could navigate as well as a sighted person. The kitchen especially intrigued him. He asked our cook endless questions. What was each implement for? He wanted to feel each one. Peixu had great patience. She showed him her knives and had him gently feel each side so that he knew which side was dull and which was sharp. Soon, he was insisting on helping her cut vegetables. I went in the kitchen one day and saw him studiously working at the cutting block. On hearing my footsteps, he exclaimed, "Look, Mama, I am cutting beans for our dinner."

From that he progressed to pounding out noodle dough and then cutting it carefully into strips by feeling the edges. Peixu let him toss the noodles he had made into the air to dry them. He was delighted with this task. He giggled as the noodles flew into the air. Peixu carefully retrieved the pieces that didn't quite make it back onto the board. Making noodles was his favorite kitchen task, but he soon became adept at doing many more things. One day he decided to find out more.

"Where do the vegetables come from?" he asked.

Peixu said, "Well in the summer they come from our garden, and we store some underground during the winter, things like carrots and potatoes."

"I want to know about the garden," he demanded.

"All right, I'll introduce you to the gardener, but he may not want to bother with you. He is rather grumpy."

"Grumpy." Gaoxing looked puzzled.

"Yes, bothered, especially by inquisitive little children."

Gaoxing thought a minute. "I will be very quiet and very good."

Soon Gaoxing was out in the garden learning how to make things grow.

The gardener said, "You make a hole like this. Then you drop seeds in the holes, cover them over with dirt and wait. If you are patient and lucky, things will come up out of the ground."

"That is wonderful. How long do we have to wait?"

"Oh, not too long. When things sprout up I will come get you and you can feel their shape. Then you will know them from the weeds. The weeds must be pulled out. I'll help you learn the difference between weeds and vegetables, but you must be very gentle with the vegetables, because growing things are fragile when they are young."

"Just like my mother says babies are. You need to be careful with them."

"Yes that is true," the gardener chuckled. "And like babies we have to help the vegetables and protect them."

"Well," Gaoxing said. "We'll just wait then." And he was content to wait. "But I don't know your name. May I call you *Cai Ren?*"(vegetable man?)

The gardener laughed, "You may call me anything you like as long it is not a bad name."

"Oh no, we are friends. I could never call you anything bad."

As Gaoxing grew, he learned all about vegetables. He also learned about the chickens, rabbits and hogs that Cai Ren took care of.

He was very busy with Master Yang and Cai Ren; Feng also tried to make his life exciting. One day when I had him to myself, I tried something different.

I said, "Would you like to build a kite?"

I helped him feel all the tiny pieces of paper that had to be made in order to fashion a dragon. We made the supports. He helped me glue them together and then add the paper. Finally, he felt the finished kite.

"So this is what a dragon is like. Now what?" he wanted to know.

"Well," I said, "real dragons are much bigger; they breathe fire and have very scaly skin. We'll add a string to the kite and hope for a windy day. We can make the dragon fly in the air."

Two days later he woke up and said, "There is wind, good wind!" We rushed into the meadow.

"Now keep the string rolled in a ball and let it out slowly when you feel the kite pulled by the wind," I said.

"Oh, I can feel it. It wants to go into the air now. Should I let it?"

"Just stay in the meadow," I said, "so the kite doesn't get snagged in a tree."

"I can feel what it wants to do. Now it wants to go to the right. Oh, no, it has turned the other way. It is hard to make it behave. But it is wonderful. I wish I could be up there with it."

Every night I either read to Gaoxing or told him a story. He was fascinated by the life of Zheng He. Zheng was a eunuch who was appointed commander of a huge fleet by the Emperor in 1421. His task was to travel around the world to find treasure and exotic things. Zhu Di, his emperor, commissioned 1,681 new ships. Among them were many gigantic nine-masted 'treasure ships' which could haul great quantities of valuable goods in their holds. One thousand three-hundred and fifty patrol ships and the same number of combat vessels accompanied the main ships. Larger war ships and four hundred freighters for transporting grain, water and horses were also part of the fleet.

Gaoxing was enthralled. "Who could even count that many ships? How big were they?"

I replied, "Some of them were even bigger than our house."

"Really?" he sighed. "I would love to have been on his voyage!"

He ran to tell Cai Ren about the fleet. Several days later Cai Ren appeared with two small boats, just the right size to float in our pond. He had even fashioned masts and sails out of old cloth and sticks. Xiao Gaoxing handled them and was delighted.

"How can we sail them in the pond?" he asked. "They might sail away from us."

"Not if we attach a long string to them like you did with your kite," Cai Ren replied, "I suppose the cabbages in the garden can wait for a time while we sail the boats. The cabbages aren't going anywhere."

"But they might sprout legs and just walk off." Gaoxing laughed hard at his own joke.

"Well, if they do, I will scold them properly," Cai Ren replied.

Soon I could hear the clunk of the boats in battle on the pond. Finally, the battle had to be interrupted for an afternoon nap. Before he went to sleep Gaoxing said, "I don't know why Peixu thinks that our gardener is grumpy."

During the following years, visits from Wu became less frequent. I knew that he had been sent to provinces farther west. Still, I felt quite neglected. However, the days were pleasant, and Master Yang had arrived. I was very pleased with the progress Gaoxing made with him. He showed Gaoxing how to move his arm across a flat surface to make strokes for characters. Gaoxing was delighted to learn that words could be represented. Next, Master Yang devised squares by gluing pieces of straw to cloths. He had Gaoxing trace out different characters inside the squares. Finally, when Master Yang felt sure that Gaoxing had memorized the feel and placement of a number of these characters, it was time to use a real brush and ink inside the squares.

"Dip the brush gently in the ink. The squares will help, but soon you will learn to do without squares."

It took days of practice before my son could write a whole page without the squares so that it looked like it had been written by a person who could see. Eventually, he began copying the poems of Li Bai and Du Fu as Master Yang read them to him.

Wu had always ignored our son. It was as if Wu could pretend that he had no blind son, only the sons he had sired with his wife in Peking. Gaoxing could sense Wu's feelings. He stayed out of Wu's way and tried to make himself invisible. He never called Wu 'Baba'. And Wu never spoke his name.

One of the rare times Wu was here with us, I called to Gaoxing.

"Come, show your father how well you can write."

Wu frowned and looked at me as though I was crazy. "Impossible!" he growled.

I was trembling, but I persisted. "Please give him a chance to show you." It galled me to beg.

Gaoxing came into the room reluctantly. Master Yang set his brush and paper up quickly and began to dictate to him. Soon Gaoxing was so absorbed in his task that he had forgotten the silent presence watching. I studied Wu's face closely and was triumphant to see the look of amazement he showed.

Wu nodded to me. "I am impressed," he whispered. "He seems to be accomplished in spite of his handicap."

I was angry that Wu had used the word 'handicap' when Gaoxing could hear him, but Gaoxing gave off an air of confidence that he had never before shown in front of his father.

CHAPTER 12

One of the most important things to happen to Gaoxing was being called by Cai Ren to come witness the birth of piglets to one of the sows. Of course he couldn't see what was happening, but Cai Ren described the whole process to him. Gaoxing could hear the grunts and bellows the sow made. Four piglets emerged, but one was much smaller than the rest. Cai Ren pointed this out. "Its mother may not want to bother with her."

Gaoxing said, "Please, may I hold her?"

Cai Ren rinsed the little piglet off in the water trough. Then he handed the piglet to Gaoxing. He said, "Here, can you hold it?"

Gaoxing held the wiggling bundle close. "Oh, please may I keep it? I will take the best care ever of it."

I had joined the others to watch the birth. I was reluctant to say yes to Gaoxing's request, but it was hard to deny my son anything.

"All right, but you must promise me several things. The first is that she cannot come into the house if she is dirty. The second is that you will be like her mother. Feed her. Teach her that she must not make a mess in the house, and finally, protect her."

Gaoxing took my pronouncements very seriously. He began bathing her in our pond every day. I hadn't forbidden him to let her in the house. Soon, I found her sleeping beside him. They both seemed extremely contented that way. He named her 'Ping' (apple).

Wu began to appreciate what Gaoxing could do even though he was blind, but Wu didn't believe me when I told him that

74

our son seemed to possess an extraordinarily attuned sense of his surroundings and could sometimes see into the future.

"I don't believe you," Wu said. He looked at me as though he thought I was mad.

Later, Wu visited us at our compound. Everyone had fallen into that deep sleep that often comes just before dawn. Gaoxing burst into our bedchamber and began shouting, "Mama! Baba! Get up now. You must come outside quickly."

I sat up on the *kong* and stared at him.

Wu gave a half grumbling noise. "How dare you come in here? Go away," he yelled.

"No Mama, please come. Something bad is going to happen."

As I listened, I didn't hear the usual night sounds. It was eerily quiet, but in a few minutes, I heard the horses making strange noises in the paddock and hitting the wooden walls frantically with their hooves. The other animals had also started to make frightened sounds. Gaoxing grabbed my hand and pulled me towards the door. I ran back and reached for Wu. All our servants and Wu's men were also rushing outside with questioning looks of awe on their faces. I didn't realize until we were clear of our home that Gaoxing held his piglet in one arm and clutched my hand with his free hand. Almost immediately the ground began to roll under our feet as though someone was shaking out a gigantic carpet.

Wu held us tightly in his arms, our son, the trembling piglet and me, as we tried to balance on our feet. Several trees in the distant woods cracked and fell with a crash. We saw the back walls of our compound where Wu and I had been sleeping heave and then crumble into a pile of rubble. I looked to my side and saw the water in the pond sway back and forth like water in a bowl which was being tipped. People began shouting and crying. I could see our cook Peixu held tightly in the arms of the gardener. They stood under a swaying tree burying their heads in each others' shoulders.

Someone cried out, "The gods must be angry!"

It was as if we all stopped breathing. A final mighty roll came and the ground heaved again. We could see a large crack spreading out at the edge of the meadow. It was so enormous that a team of horses could have fallen into it. Then everything was still again. Only with the calm, did I begin to shake like a puppet being held by a master puppeteer. Even Wu looked pale. Ping made soft mewing noises like a kitten, but Xiao Gaoxing looked unfazed.

"I told you, Mama. I'm so glad you came outside."

Wu looked quite disturbed when he saw the rubble in the corner where we had been sleeping, but all he said was, "We'll have to have the repairs started right away."

Everyone walked around aimlessly until Wu barked orders to his men to begin clearing the rubble immediately. The sun rose with its comforting warmth while we tried to restore the rhythm of a normal routine. Everyone was fearful for the rest of the day, but no aftershocks occurred. Wu made no acknowledgement of Gaoxing's role in our escape, but I did notice him glancing at Gaoxing more thoughtfully. Wu was not a man who believed in omens, seers, or shamans. However, he said, "I will just stay here with you another night."

It was comforting to have him there; though, even he, could not protect us from earthquakes. The men drank more than usual that evening. Everyone stayed awake far into the night except for Gaoxing, who lay sleeping, peacefully, with Ping in his arms.

CHAPTER 13

I could usually hear Wu's approach to our home because of the clatter of the hoof beats of his retinue. He always brought a small contingent of his men with him. It was for his protection and mine. I stood at the south gate with anticipation. When he came in, he lifted me and spun me around.

"I have been asked to go to the capital—some sort of award from the emperor."

"That's wonderful. When do you go?"

"I must leave right away."

I felt terribly crestfallen. I managed a half-hearted mumble. "Oh, will you be coming back soon?"

He smiled. "How would you and Gaoxing like to visit Peking for a short time? You couldn't stay with me, but my father's home, which was partially burned by Li Zicheng, is somewhat restored, at least enough so that you could be comfortable there. Several of my father's servants, who fled, begged me to allow them to return there to start repairs and keep order in the house. I will instruct them to treat you well."

I could barely contain my excitement. I had heard wonderful stories about the capital and the Forbidden City.

"Of course," I replied, "I would like that very much. Would I be able to see the Forbidden City?"

"I will give you a pass through the west gate into the city. My father's home is a small distance from the west of the city. Once you are in Peking, you will be amazed at the vastness of the city. If you pack your things quickly, you can go with us now."

I was flustered. I knew I must hurry. Wu was not a patient man. What did I need for myself and Gaoxing? I rushed around grabbing this and that, not taking time to even wonder how one dressed in the capital city.

I yelled to Gaoxing who was practicing calligraphy. "Come quickly, your father is taking us to Peking."

He rushed in with a questioning look on his face. "Now?" he said. "Right now?"

"Yes, be quick. Our horses are waiting outside. I have your clothes."

I don't even remember the trip there. My head was full of questions and fantasies.

How should I behave? What would his father's house be like? Would the servants listen to a woman they didn't know, especially one with big feet? Before I knew it, we had entered the walled gates of the city. Wu gave a cursory glance toward one of the parapets. I froze remembering that his father's severed head had been displayed high on one of the walls; however, Wu remained composed. We made our way through a seemingly endless warren of streets, through the west gates, and a short distance beyond them, to his father's house.

"Here we are," Wu said.

In front of us was an imposing structure, but I could see the darkened sections of the walls where they had been burned and also the new construction which replaced part of the house.

I held my breath. Finally I found my voice. "Oh, it is even grander than I had imagined."

Wu just smiled. "My father was a general too. But I'm afraid neither of us got to spend much time here."

The servants clustered around the entrance curious to see Wu's new concubine and their son.

"This is Lady Bourtai. She and my son will be staying here for a while. Treat them well."

'Lady?' 'My son?' The words were sweet to my ears. I had not heard us being described by Wu before.

The servants stole a quick glance at my feet and I think most of them registered that Gaoxing was blind, but then they all immediately *kowtowed* very low towards us.

"Things will go very well here I assume," Wu said with a severe warning look.

We were thus installed and made quite comfortable in his father's house. Gaoxing asked me to help him orient himself through the house after the servants had gone to bed. We were a strange pair feeling the walls and walking a few paces to the furniture in each room whispering to each other.

"Could we do it all again Mama? I need to memorize things in my mind."

So we retraced our steps and went through the rooms again with me holding a small candle and Gaoxing grasping one of my hands and feeling the surfaces of objects with his other hand.

"There are some places that we won't need to go like the servants' quarters and even the kitchen. Remember, you are not at home with Peixu. You might not be welcome in the kitchen."

He just nodded.

We finally went to bed. I chose to have Gaoxing stay in the same room with me. He was as much a comfort to me as I was to him. We whispered throughout the night and were exhausted when morning came and a servant entered to wake us for breakfast. The food was quite different. It was much richer. We had more dishes of various kinds, and there were some new things we had never tasted before.

After a few days, we were more familiar with the place. I was overcome by curiosity about Peking. One of the servants mentioned in an offhand way that Wu's wife and son lived near the west wall. How I would like to see them with my own eyes! What would they be like? How did *they* live? I supposed his *real* home would be more splendid than this.

Soon I began taking walks while Gaoxing took his afternoon nap. I went through the west gate. I had a crude map which one of the servants had been kind enough to make for me.

I was a bit anxious. "Will you be all right while I'm gone?" I asked Gaoxing. "I would like to see as much of the city as I can."

"Of course, Mama—and you can describe everything to me when you come back."

I was good with directions, but didn't go far the first day. I even made myself a more detailed map. Each day I ventured through new streets. The city was marvelous and it seemed endless. There were vegetable and meat vendors at some places and shops where silk could be bought in other places. The merchants seemed to cluster together by the type of goods that they sold even as they did in Shenyang. I dressed plainly so that no one paid much attention to me. By chatting with people, I finally learned where Wu's family lived. Well, it couldn't hurt just to look at the place. When I got to their street, I was confronted by the high wall of their home. It had a large red door at the entry, but I learned no secrets just by looking at it. A Muslim cemetery was nearby. There were big arches guarding its entry. I walked through it. Then I had an idea. I could hide behind one of the cemetery arches and watch the red door. Surely, someone would come out, maybe even Wu's wife or son.

"So, what did you discover today, Mama?"

I always picked out one new thing to tell Xiao Gaoxing.

"I visited an elaborate family temple today. The large Buddha was made of real gold. Oh, the wealth of this city is amazing even though it was recently sacked by Li's men."

"I would love to be able to feel the Buddha. Could we go together some time?"

I felt guilty, especially for the time I spent away from Gaoxing when I watched Wu's home. Gaoxing was lonely. I was the only resource he had in this strange place.

"Very soon," I said, "just let me become a little more familiar with this area and make sure it is safe."

Gaoxing sighed, but he seemed to be content with my answer.

The next day, I took up my usual stance hiding behind one of the arches of the cemetery. The red door opened and a servant began walking toward me instead of toward the shops. I was petrified. There was nothing I could do but remain hidden behind the arch. He came to the arch and stopped.

Without looking directly at me he said, "My mistress knows of your curiosity. She would like to meet you. Will you follow me?"

I felt like a child. I had no will of my own. I just followed him through the red door, around the spirit wall, across a beautiful courtyard and up three steps to the main hall. The woman, who I knew must be Wu's wife, was sitting calmly in a chair facing me. It would have been impolite for me to stare. I *kowtowed* without saying anything. Then I stole a quick glance at her. She wasn't what I had expected. She was much older than I and was a rather homely woman, but she seemed kindly and dignified.

"Should I guess why you have seen fit to spy on my household?"

I was totally embarrassed. "Please forgive me. Curiosity is one of my most bothersome traits. I am one of Wu's servants."

"You don't look like a servant, even in those clothes." She looked at my feet. "Might you be a Manchu? I have heard that the general was given a Manchu princess recently."

I lowered my head. How she must hate me. "Yes, I am one of his …"

I couldn't finish.

"Concubines," she said. "Don't be afraid. I have no ill will toward you. I am happy just to be here with my family. Peking is an interesting place and friends visit me. I rarely see the general; although he visits regularly when he is in Peking to see our children, especially his eldest son, Wu Cheng."

Of course, eldest sons were almost always favored by their fathers. It was a matter of pride and a Chinese tradition. I looked beyond this woman and saw a young man hovering in the doorway to the next room.

Without looking around, Wu's wife motioned him forward. "Come in. You must meet your father's new concubine."

I had never thought of myself as a concubine. The boy entered the room and fixed me with a hostile stare.

"Where are your manners?" his mother admonished sharply. "*Kowtow* to the lady and don't look so grim. She seems to be gentle. She won't hurt you."

He stole a glance at my feet. There was a faint look of disgust on his face.

His mother noticed. "She is a Manchu. They don't bind their womens' feet. I also happen to know that she is a Manchu princess. There is no reason that we can't get to know her. She doesn't seem as vain or spoiled as Chen Yuan Yuan is."

I gasped at her mention of the famous Chen Yuan Yuan. This woman seemed to know everything, even though she was confined to this house with her bound feet.

She smiled at me. "I also know that you have a son, blind but very talented. Perhaps you could bring him to meet me and his stepbrother some day."

The young man looked startled by her words, but his expression became a little more accepting.

"I would like that very much. My name is Bourtai and my son's name is Wu Gaoxing."

"My name is Ping Hua. You may call me that if you like."

I again *kowtowed* to her and then backed away. I didn't know what else to say to her. I felt very awkward.

"I will bring my son here some day."

When I sensed that I was near the door, I turned and fled. I couldn't wait to tell Gaoxing the news. But how could I explain my interview with Wu's wife? I mulled it over as I returned slowly. I would think of something!

I never did manage to take Gaoxing to see Wu's family. After the short time we spent in Peking, we returned to Jinzhou. Wu had permission from the emperor to stay in Jinzhou to put his affairs in order before he returned to Shanxi Province where he was now assigned. Because we both knew that the emperor could post him anywhere in the future, we agreed that I would stay in Jinzhou with Wu Gaoxing. All generals were called to the capital annually, so we hoped that the emperor would also give Wu time to travel to see us, but I was skeptical.

I said, "Your family is in Peking. Why would the emperor allow you to travel here?"

Wu just laughed, "The emperor gives his generals time. He can't be expected to follow me around."

"But you won't have time to do everything. The trip to Jinzhou and then back to Peking is not an easy one."

I was thinking of him visiting his wife and also Chen Yuan Yuan, his celebrated concubine, but I didn't say this.

"I will come to Jinzhou as often as I can. Don't worry. If I am assigned to a permanent post, then you can come stay with me. My wife and children are being held as hostages in Peking to ensure that I remain loyal to the Emperor. He considers that I will want to return to Peking to see them. I can return to my post by any route." Again he laughed.

So it was that Gaoxing and I remained in the east while Wu was sent to a different post in Sichuan. I missed Wu with a physical yearning, but was otherwise content with enjoying the almost daily changes in Gaoxing under the tutoring of Master Yang. We became a family of sorts with Master Yang being like a grandfather to Gaoxing and Feng taking the place of an older brother.

CHAPTER 14

During the years after our trip to Peking, Wu's assignments took him further and further away from Jinzhou. Even though he was recalled to Peking once a year by the emperor in order to ascertain his loyalty, I saw him much less frequently. This saddened me a great deal, but, otherwise, my life was pleasant and peaceful. I spent most of my time with Gaoxing. I also painted water colors and practiced my singing skills. The *erhu* was an instrument I learned to play when I was younger, so I made it part of our daily ritual. Gaoxing was happy when I played for him.

One day he said, "Mama, I like to hear you play and sing, but I would like to be able to play the *erhu* too."

I consulted with Feng and Master Yang.

Master Yang said, "It shouldn't be too difficult to make an *erhu* using yours as a pattern. We need to find the same kind of wood, the same kind of strings and the special material for the bow."

Feng became animated. "I could look for all those things. I'm sure I could find them in Shenyang."

I knew he would make any excuse to go to Shenyang, because that was where Mei Hua was. While he was searching there for the materials we needed, he came across a *pipa,* a sort of a gourd-like instrument with strings he could pluck. He was delighted with his find, and couldn't wait to return and show us. However, he needed to make a side trip to make sure that Mei Hua was doing well. Mei Hua was learning to play the flute. No one instructed her. She taught herself and was already an accomplished musician.

Feng decided that he would learn to play the *pipa* to accompany her. He stayed much longer than he said he would; consequently, I was alternatively worried about him or angry with him. Finally, he returned trailing apologies with him like a dog's tail.

"Feng," I said, "you have worried me so. Why did you stay so long?"

It appeared that he and Mei Hua were forming a strong attachment to each other.

He said, "I told her I wasn't a whole man. She understood and told me that she would always be my little sister and love me just as I am."

I was happy for both of them; it is difficult to be alone in the world.

Later, in 1659, the counselors for Fulin, the Shun Chi Emperor, advised him that the establishment of three feudatories would result in more stability in the remote southern areas of China where many powerful people were still in favor of restoring the lost Ming Empire. Fulin established the Three Feudatories that were called *San Fan* and were to be administered by three prominent generals who were loyal to the new Qing rule. The three were Shang Kexi, Geng Zhongming and Wu San Gui. These men now had semi-independent rule over the provinces which the emperor appointed to each of them as their fiefdom.

Wu was elated and sent me a message to join him in Kunming. He said it would be a permanent home for both of us. He wanted me to come there as soon as I could. I was excited. Immediately, I traveled to Shenyang to try to persuade Mamu and her household to join us.

"Mamu," I said, "Kunming is known as a place of eternal spring. You would feel much better there than here in Shenyang with its bitter winters—no aches and pains. Wu will provide handsomely for us. We can be so happy there together!"

Mamu looked stunned. "I couldn't leave Shenyang, the place where I was born, and what of Mei Hua? General Wu might remember when you went off to have a baby. He told you he would kill the child if he found out who it was."

"Oh Mamu, Wu won't remember what year Mei Hua was born. He will accept her as the daughter of Girten, and then think no more about it. He is a man of the moment. She will be safe. Master Yang could come with us. And you would get a real chance to know Gaoxing. Please say you will come!"

Mamu's face was drawn. "I may be too old to travel that distance." She hesitated, "I'm not sure I could make the trip, but Goaxing *is* my great- grandson."

"Please, Mamu. Think about it over night. Wu has enough money to make sure our travels are as comfortable as possible. I could hire bearers to carry you in a sedan chair."

She went to bed, but I stayed up worrying myself about the difficulties of making a trip of such distance. When I was studying with Master Yang, he had given me a map of Manchuria and also a more primitive map of China. As I compared the distance from Shenyang to Peking, and then looked at the distance between Shenyang and Kunming, I grew doubtful about Mamu being able to survive the trip. So many mountains and rivers to cross! When I thought about the rivers, a plan began to grow in my mind. Perhaps we could travel south on the Grand Canal. Then we would travel west by way of the Chang Jiang (Yangtze River). I knew that the river flowed in the opposite direction from the way we wanted to travel, but I had heard of trackers, pole men and porters, who pulled boats up the river. That would have to be our plan. Finally satisfied that I had a viable plan to present to Mamu, I decided to let the next day be my day of persuasion. I outlined my plan to Mamu, Girten and Master Yang. They agreed, but Mamu was still reluctant to say yes. We finally persuaded her to agree.

"Oh, Mamu," I said, "There will be so many wonders to see along our way. You have made me so happy, and going by boat will be much easier for all of us."

I wrote to Wu and sent him my plan by post horse.

After many days, Wu's reply came. "Your plan is most reasonable. I will contact various territorial commanders to help you. They can provide food, soldiers for safety or anything else you might need. Come soon."

Gaoxing came into the room hesitantly. "I don't suppose she can go with us," he said.

Who? Ping of course, his pet pig. I had been so busy planning that I had forgotten to settle things where we were.

"We can ask Cai Ren to take care of her. I'm truly sorry, but we can't take her with us," I answered.

Cai Ren was glad to agree.

And the house? I had also forgotten about it in my excitement. I decided to see if Cai Ren and Peixi would like to live there as caretakers. If I or my family wanted to come back, the place would be available. They were very happy with this plan. While I lived in Jinzhou, I felt like the independent woman I always wanted to be, but I realized that this feeling was one of false independence. After all, the good life we had there was because of Wu's money.

I arranged for a wagon to take us to the uppermost station of the Grand Canal at Tongzhou. I expected that this would be the hardest part of the trip for Mamu, and it was. Wu sent me many silver taels to use for the trip. I decided that we needed to stay the night in Tongzhou. Mamu could sleep comfortably for the night while I made arrangements for our trip down the Grand Canal. We also had a separate wagon with our possessions. We brought it on the trip so far. I knew it couldn't go by water to Kunming; still, the cost of overland travel would be extremely expensive.

I paid half of the cost for the wagon to travel by land to Kunming. Wu guaranteed the second half of the payment when the wagon arrived. But who knew when that would be?

We did take our musical instruments on the canal boat along with a change of clothes and rice cakes and cucumbers to sustain us in an emergency.

As we arrived at the dock and looked at our boat, Mamu exclaimed, "Oh, it's so small. How will we manage?"

I was a little sharp with her. I was not about to change our plans now. I was new to this way of traveling, but I determined to pretend that this was just an ordinary trip. The captain helped us into the boat, and we found that it did have enough room for all of us, but just barely. We had a roof over our heads. The boatmen stayed in a very small shack-like hut at one end of the boat. Most of the time they were out in the open, unless there was a hard rain. A tiny cooking stove stood at the very end of the boat.

The head boatman said, "We can cook rice, vegetables and a small amount of meat when it isn't raining."

We each had a pallet as our personal space under the covered part of the boat. I had to admit that it wasn't the greatest arrangement. I mentioned to the boatman that we were invited by Wu San Gui to visit him in Kunming. Wu's name was known throughout the empire; consequently, the boatman looked impressed. This was the reaction I had hoped for, because I had sewn many silver taels and a number of smaller denominations in my cloak and also into a belt with small pockets. I was pleased by his tone of deference. It meant that he and his men would not dare attempt to rob us. It also meant that we would be treated well. I was a bit devious with my family. I found out ahead of time what we might see next, because I often went to stand beside one of the boatmen to find out what to expect in each stage of the trip. The captain treated me like a younger sister. He explained about the parts of the Grand Canal we would come to next.

He said, "We'll soon be coming to a set of locks which will either raise or lower the boat according to where it needs to be for the next section of the canal. You'll find the locks very interesting."

He was kind and willing to answer my questions, but he seemed to feel sorry for us. I sensed that he was somewhat doubtful that all of us could make such a long journey.

Mamu stayed on her pallet most of the time. This worried me greatly. I did everything I could think of to make her comfortable. The rest of us were fascinated by the canal. Mei Hua and Feng found most of the scenery we passed fascinating. They sat at the side of the boat oohing and awing at all the sights. Where the dikes on either side of the canal were perpendicular, rows of children, with their legs hanging over the edge of the dike, sat at the canal end of the streets that ran up to the dikes. They waved and called out to us. At a very short distance behind them, we could see the entrances to their homes. At certain places, the canal was quite wide. At these places, we could see boats traveling in the opposite direction from us. We could look either behind us or ahead of us to see boats following in a line which looked like segments of a long sinuous snake.

Courier stations every 35-45 kilometers had soldiers at each station to help locals maintain and repair the canal.

When we came to the first lock, Feng, Girten, Mei Hua, and Gaoxing were excited and very curious. The boatman explained to us how the locks worked. Gaoxing could feel the boat rising up or going down. He absorbed every thing the boatman said about the locks.

"Mama," he said. "I can picture the way the Grand Canal works and I enjoy hearing the shouts and greetings of the people on the sides of the dikes. The engineers who planned the canal must have been truly brilliant."

I certainly agreed.

I knew about the marvelous silks from Suzhou which were thinner and more beautifully designed than silks from any other place. I asked the boatman if we could stop there for just an hour or two.

He said, "I have seen these silks and they are truly marvelous, but we'll not be going that far down the canal."

I looked disappointed.

Seeing my look he said, "There is a place near where you will be transferring to the Yangtze River. We can make a brief stop there. A small selection of silk from the Suzhou area is at Guazhou. You might find something you would like there."

When we came to a spot from which an interesting temple or another special scene could be viewed, the head boatman moved our boat out of the line of traffic so that we had more than a fleeting glimpse of the area. Then, I persuaded Mamu to come to the side of the boat so that she would be able to see the unique view. After she had seen these different places, she became more interested in our trip. Finally, we arrived at Guazhou. I asked her to describe what she saw to Gaoxing. She was more observant when she knew she would be relating the scenes to Gaoxing.

The boat stopped there long enough for us to shop and also eat dinner on land. I over-indulged in buying silk, though I knew it would crowd my pallet, but I thought it might be the last time I would see such wonderful material. We re-boarded long enough for us to go through a slip which took us to the boat we would take up the Yangtze River. Our captain and his boatman had been so helpful that I gave him a large bonus for himself and his crew.

We were excited about the next part of our journey. The new river boats were larger than the one we had been in, so each of us had a little more space. We didn't expect our boat to be conveyed the way it was. We had watched as pole men moved our boat from the center of the Grand Canal to one side or the other depending on where various rocks or other obstacles were in our path. We were able to see much of the countryside along the Grand Canal. Often, this was not so on the Yangtze. Much of the earth on either side of the river rose in high cliffs on both sides of the river.

We stopped at Wuhan where I bought a large butterfly kite on the river front. The kite was as tall as Gaoxing. We played our musical instruments on deck in the evening.

Beyond Wuhan, the river widened, and for a little while, we could see the countryside on either side of the river. Our boat had pole men similar to the ones who were on the Grand Canal, but their poles were heavier and sturdier than the canal poles had been. As we progressed, we often came to docks placed right against the high walls of the surrounding cliffs. When we were in between two cliffs, it felt as though we were confined in a dark hole. Sometimes we pulled up to one of these docks at dusk and spent the night with our boat tethered to the dock. I felt we were safe, because no one was likely to make such a precipitous approach to our boat. Also, one of the boat men was always on watch during the night.

In addition to the pole men, our captain occasionally used a sail to move us if the wind was behind us. The most astonishing method used to move us forward was done by naked men who pulled the boat forward by using ropes. They struggled along paths parallel to the river that were hanging on the sides of mountains and cliffs. The plank paths were supported by stakes driven into the sides of the cliffs. The trackers were usually bent over almost in half from the efforts they made. We thought these men were a pitiful sight. I ventured to ask our captain why they wore no clothes.

"The ropes would rasp and leave festering sores," the captain said. "This way although the ropes bite into their skin, they do not develop incurable wounds."

I knew I had led a sheltered life, but I wasn't so unworldly as to believe there was little sorrow in my fellow countrymen's lives, yet I had never come face to face with the abject despair our trackers lived with day after day.

Mei Hua found the naked trackers especially fascinating.

Mamu said, "You shouldn't let her watch those men all day. It isn't moral." Girten and I just grinned.

Girten said, "But Mamu, this is a harmless way for her to learn about the world." We both knew that Mei Hua was also learning about the wretched conditions of people in her world and what naked men looked like.

As we approached Chongqing, we could see terraced farms running up the nearby mountains. We did stop in Chongqing for a short time while we climbed to a high point overlooking the river.

As our captain said, "The view from the Gates to the Sky is superb. I can tie the boat here if you like. And you are fairly close to Dazu. Marvelous Buddhist carvings can be seen there both inside and outside the caves."

Master Yang's ears perked up. He quickly turned to me and asked, "Would it be possible to go there?"

I was the one in a hurry, but Dazu might be a place we could all remember. Master Yang had done so much for me and Gaoxing. I couldn't turn down his request.

"All right," I said. "Let me talk to the captain to make sure our boat will be safe."

I promised the captain extra money for the time he and his men would spend there. A small bonus would be included. He assured me that he would guard the boat with his life.

"And you will not leave us?" I asked.

"Never," he replied.

We were in a festive mood as we prepared for our excursion. I didn't bother with hiring horses. We could all travel on a wagon for a short time. The trip would take two or three days, but it would give us a much needed break from our life on the boat. I knew that I must wear my cloak even though it was far too hot. Trust only went so far. The amount of money sewn in the cloak had to last until the end of our travels.

Walking on land felt strange after our long confinement on boats. Mamu had the most difficulty. Feng guided her gently and slowly.

Our cart took us directly to the carvings at Baoding Shan. Amazingly, Daoist, Buddhist and Confucian carvings were intermixed in great variety. The first thing I took Gaoxing to was a huge carving of a reclining Buddha. I walked him from one end of the carving to the other, describing it as well as I could. We then went to a carving of a thousand-armed Guanyin whose arms flickered like flames in the sunlight.

Gaoxing said, "This is one of the times I most regret that I can not see. Your descriptions have helped me picture these wonders. The reclining Buddha was so very long. It must have taken artisans months or years to carve it."

One extraordinary set of carvings depicted Buddhist hell where the Buddha and bodisattvas looked down on drunken sinners who were being ravaged by demons that had wild heads of voracious animals. I found it to be rather ridiculous, but Mamu took it seriously.

I said, "Mamu, even if this pictures reality, you would have nothing to fear. You are one of the most virtuous women in China." She was pleased by what I said.

At a nearby restaurant, we stuffed ourselves with the kinds of foods we couldn't get on the boat. One of the boatmen served as our guide. He told the owner of the restaurant about the musical presentations we made on the boat. The restaurant owner said, "I would be honored if your group would play for us."

"I'm sorry, but we don't have our instruments with us," I said.

In a flurry of people rushing around, instruments like ours appeared as if from nowhere. We enjoyed performing for a large audience. The audience was very receptive, so much so, that we were cheered for the next stage of our journey.

CHAPTER 15

We took a small tributary from the Yangtze River southward. When we were not too far from Kunming, we left the river to begin the last leg of our journey by land. Again, I negotiated for a wagon, a sedan chair for Mamu and fresh horses. We were about sixty *li* from Kunming when we saw a group approaching on horseback. As the group grew closer, I recognized Long Qiong in the lead. I was glad to see him, but was quite disappointed that Wu wasn't with him. Long's men helped us further with our possessions. To my surprise, Long said that our overland wagon was already there.

Mamu was relieved that the air was more pleasant than it had been toward the end of the river trip. Speaking especially to Mamu, Long said, "Madam, you won't have to bear the humidity and the heat of your last days on the river. Kunming is higher than the surrounding area and is blessed with soft, beautifully scented breezes. The mountain ranges around Kunming protect it from cold winds."

Then Long said to me, "Let's ride ahead. I'll tell you about your new home. Wu sends you his apologies for not meeting you. His administrative duties have expanded much beyond Yunnan Province. He has monopolies throughout the whole southwest in salt, copper, silver, tin, sugar cane and rhubarb."

"Rhubarb?" I said, "I don't even know what that is."

"You will see; I'm sure you'll like it. It's a red plant that can be combined with sugar and boiled to make a very delicious dessert."

Long knew that I wasn't interested in hearing about desserts. I wanted to hear about Wu.

"Wu has to travel to see the governors of several provinces and also see his agents who collect his various monopolies. Most people in the area respect him, but he can't take the chance that someone might try to cheat him. So he travels into Sichuan, Guizhou and Guangxi. He has authority even in the southern parts of Shaanxi."

"Why does he want to work so hard and expand his authority so much?" I asked.

"He is more driven than ever before. Since he became the ruler of such a large territory, he has taken on an air of personal grandeur," Long replied.

We stopped for a few minutes at a pond while the horses drank. Long handed me a small purse.

"What is this?" I asked.

"Wu uses part of his copper to mint coins in small denominations. The local people have grown used to them. They are useful for small purchases. You might need the smaller coins in the next few days while you settle in. You will probably need things that no one has thought of. Wu found you and your family a fine house with a good deal of space."

"He didn't have it built did he?"

Long laughed, "No, no, but he was in luck. He purchased a large house from an older couple. Their parents died and their sons left, so they were wandering around in a house much too big for them. They wanted to sell and move into a smaller home, but they were afraid they wouldn't find a buyer for the large home. When Wu heard about them, he offered a handsome price for their house. He wants to have a room in the house where he can meet informally with some of his top advisors and generals. Plenty of extra spaces make that possible."

I was worried and asked Long whether Wu would be staying in the house with me when he was in the area.

"Most probably," Long said, "but he has a special headquarters just for himself in the northeast section of Kunming. It was previously a Daoist temple---small in size but quite grand in concept. This two-storied shrine is made almost entirely of bronze. It has screens, columns and flying eaves. The bronze is maintained by rubbing the outside with tomatoes or lemons to make it shine. Because of the shine, the temple is called the golden temple. The floor is made of extraordinary Dali marble which comes from a quarry to the north. Ancient trees surround the courtyard. It is quite beautiful." He was quiet after that as we got closer to Kunming.

We finally reached our new house. It was more than I could ever have hoped for. The floor plan was in an elongated U configuration. The back section had a second story of bedrooms across the back wall. Beneath that story on ground level was the ancestral hall with sitting rooms on either side of the hall. Three steps led up to the hall. On the lower floor, the legs of the house plan had a number of rooms running down on either side of a central court. On both sides, additional family bedrooms were near the ancestor's hall and sitting rooms. On the left side Mamu settled in one bedroom. I didn't want the stairs to be a problem for her. Girten was happy to be in the room beside hers. This side also had an eating room with a long table and beyond that a kitchen. The right side had a room for Mei Hua and several storage rooms. Beyond them were rooms for the servants. In the upstairs rooms the floors and walls were made from bamboo. A walkway of bamboo flooring outside of these rooms made it possible to go from one room to another. A railing, also of bamboo, protected people from falling from the walkway. At the front of each upstairs room, bamboo walls extended halfway up the room. Fretted windows ran the rest of the way to the ceiling. Doors to the rooms were fitted with drapes, as were the top halves of each room. Stairways to the main floor ran down on either end of the upstairs hall. The inside eaves of the house extended over our rooms so that any rain water fell into grooved channels which ran around the central court and out a drain. The eaves of the first floor also extended beyond the rooms so that rain water drained into the same channels in the central court and was also run off. Each of the two corners in the back of the dwelling had a two-story well opening inward to let light into the house. These ran from the ground to the top of the house. The house plan was excellent. I could barely wait to arrange things. I looked out of the room which was mine to see mountains in the distance with clouds moving lazily.

I settled Feng and Gaoxing in the room on the left top floor at the head of the stairs leading to the ground floor. Master Yang was in the room to their right; then I was in the central room that connected to a small sitting room to my right. The final room on the top floor was saved for the nights when Wu would be in the house. It was at the top right of the second story at the head of the right hand stairway.

Trees and fragrant wild flowers, magnolias, orchids, bougainvilleas, poppies and other mountain plants surrounded the house. The area seemed magical.

Wu had his company cook find us a good cook among the local people. The new cook had already settled himself into one of the servant's rooms. I was thankful that the cook could understand *putonghua*. All of the upstairs rooms already had beds in them. We had to forage in the storage rooms to find beds for Mamu, Girten and Mei Hua. I assured them that, in the morning, we would find better beds or have them built.

Mamu sighed, "I am happy to find any bed. The journey was longer than I ever could have imagined. I am surprised that I survived." She went abruptly into her room, and we could soon hear sounds of contented snoring.

The cook turned out to be a magician. He told me his name was Yin. It was late in the afternoon when we arrived, but we hadn't had any food since the morning, so I asked him to prepare a full meal as soon as he could. In a short time he called us. A sumptuous feast was laid out on the long table, and to my amazement stewed rhubarb was our dessert. Every one looked at the small dishes with a bit of suspicion, but soon all the bowls were empty.

Early the next morning I heard the din of many voices at a distance. I hurriedly dressed and went down to see what was happening. A strange beast with flapping ears and a very long nose came over a hillock. I could see a man on its back. A noisy crowd followed. I was afraid to get too close. I stood petrified as the animal made its way directly toward me. I saw then that it was Wu on the animal's back, but a different Wu from the one I remembered. He had the same long, full head of hair, but his body was thicker. It was still muscular but not thin. He had no shirt and no shoes on. Several bracelets encircled his arms. His legs were covered by pants made of a flowing cloth of bright colors. His skin had darkened, but the most astonishing change was his pompous air. He looked like he owned the world, and in this area, he probably did. This wasn't the man I had dreamed about for so long.

Wu maneuvered the animal beside me and said, "Join me. The view is wonderful up here. By the way, this is an elephant, a delightful beast."

He indicated that several of his men should lift me up, and in minutes I was also on the elephant's back. I gripped the seat. I was probably safe, but I didn't know whether elephants reared up on their hind legs the way horses did.

I felt a tap on my leg from Wu. I wasn't sure whether it was comforting or condescending. He turned to look at me and grinned. "We'll take a little stroll around Kunming. Most of the people here in the city have learned some *putonghua* from my soldiers, but there are many interesting minorities in the area who have a different language altogether."

"Can we visit them?"

"It's impossible for me. I'm too busy right now, but I can arrange for you and your household to go most places. It is very safe. I can't eat dinner with you tonight, but I would like you to come to my official residence later tonight. I'll send someone to guide you."

So we would be back together. It had been so long. I wasn't sure how I felt.

CHAPTER 16

I was nervous about the night to come. It would be a reunion of sorts. But what kind? I thought about the costume I made after learning the dances of the foreign women in Shenyang. I had never used the costume other than for practicing, but it would be a relief to start the evening with my dancing as a gift to Wu. This way the awkwardness between us might be less. Still, I was probably the one who felt the most distance.

After all these years, I was amazed that my costume still fit. I went to my room early in order to practice. It all came back. I could still dance with ease. I joined the evening meal with the others. The meal dragged on. I had little appetite. At dusk, a soldier on horseback appeared with a horse for me. As we came closer to Wu's headquarters, I began to feel anger towards him for the many lost years when we weren't together.

Wu found a temple called the Jin Dian in the northeastern part of Kunming very impressive. At one time, the temple had been a Daoist place of worship. Now, Wu was having it restored as his headquarters. Wu came out to talk to the soldier; then he turned to me and said, "I have arranged for him to come back at sunrise to return you to your home."

I was caught by surprise. We had not spent the entire night together for a long time. Different emotions were tumbling around in my head. As the soldier and I approached Wu's headquarters, I thought about my life. My whole family and I were dependent on Wu. What would I be without him? I was pampered, and I was used to it. I realized that I couldn't risk alienating him. Fortunately, I was able to express my anger in the dance. I danced faster and with more feeling than I ever expressed before. Wu was mesmerized.

He just stared at me for a moment. Finally, he said, "You are a woman of many talents and surprises. Fortunately, I like surprises of this kind."

He pulled me down with him on his pallet. Our reunion was violent. It seemed to satisfy a need for both of us. I had rarely spent the whole night with Wu. Afterwards, it was very comforting to lie in his arms and feel his warmth. I would have liked to talk, but he fell asleep quickly. It was not long before I fell into a dreamless sleep. Morning came too soon. Wu was gone, but his soldier was waiting, and the ride back to my new house was exceptional. I turned to look at the temple; it dazzled as the sun was coming up. The rice fields were a brilliant green and the fields of rapeseed shone like gold.

The previous evening, Wu said, "I will be very busy the next few days. I must talk to the governor of Yunnan about problems at my copper mines. You can find much to interest you here. If you like, you could visit some of the minorities. It will be quite safe. I'll assign an interpreter to go with you. Check with Long Qiong. He takes care of all my business when I am away."

"What does Xi Chu do?" I asked.

"Xi Chu is in charge of the soldiers. He makes sure that they remain in good fighting shape. When I return we can take a small trip. To the east of Kunming is the Stone Forest which is amazing. We might even go to Dali. You will find the marble quarries fascinating. We can also see the cormorants."

Cormorants? Were they another minority? Or maybe they were fish in the river. I didn't want to show my ignorance by asking.

I purposely forgot about Xi Chu. I was in no hurry to see him again. I had listened to his counsel to Wu on the many evenings when they all sat at our table. I opposed his ideas and his way of thinking. He thought that any problem could be resolved by violence.

I went to Long Qiong with my request to visit several of the minority groups.

He said, "The Miao are a colorful people. If you don't mind, I will go with you, but I can't be away from here too long, so I will find an interpreter to stay with you if you want to stay more than one day. The Miao are friendly and generous. They make beautiful silver jewelry and the women wear caps decorated with hanging fringes of silver which dangle all around their heads. The headdresses make lovely sounds when they move. Would all of your household like to go with us?"

It was an excellent idea. At dinner I invited everyone. The enthusiasm was great except for Mamu.

She said, "I am comfortable right here. I'll look forward to hearing all about your visit when you come back."

I didn't try to persuade her. Our journey had been very hard for her. She was entitled just to sit now that she was older. That evening, our dinner table was lively in anticipation of a new exploration.

Long arrived early in the morning. All of us were ready and eager to go. When we reached our destination, I was dazzled by the appearance of the Miao women. Some wore a number of silver bracelets. Most had extremely large silver disks draped around their necks and had pendants which reached below their breasts. They offered us bananas and elephant yams accompanied by spicy rice patties which had been cooked in wrapped leaves. We were fascinated by the intricacy of the women's silver bracelets.

We gathered with the women in a common area. We could see that most of their houses were wooden, ranging up the hillsides with small vegetable patches and rice paddies interspersed between them. Much larger community rice paddies were being cultivated by the men that day; however, the women usually worked the rice fields too.

Mei Hua was fascinated by the silver jewelry. She said, "I would love to learn how to make such beautiful things."

Immediately, our interpreter went to a group of the women. We didn't understand what they were saying, but it soon became clear that he had asked if they would teach us how to make bracelets like theirs. Feng, Mei Hua, and even Gaoxing were excited by this idea. I finally had to admit that I would enjoy learning, but what about the silver? Long assured me that he could pay for any silver we might use. I was dubious about Gaoxing being able to join the lessons, but I didn't say anything. He must have felt my anxiousness.

He said, "Mama, you know when I am determined, I can learn anything. Don't worry."

We were given strands of silver. Then we watched how the patterns of the bracelets were made. One of the women, who realized that Gaoxing would have difficulty, guided his hands so that he would learn the patterns. The day passed swiftly. As we fashioned our bracelets, we also learned a smattering of the Miao language while the women tried to learn some of ours. Because of the large company of Wu's soldiers in the area, most people in the province already knew a few words of *putonghua*.

Long said, "I can't leave the garrison too long, but I can arrange for you to stay here until tomorrow evening if you like."

I answered, "Yes, we would like to stay."

Long said, "I'll go back to Kunming tonight and arrange for someone to come late tomorrow afternoon to escort you back. Perhaps you might want to buy more strands of silver so that you can experiment with designs when you are back in Kunming."

Immediately he pulled out some coins and began to bargain with the women.

The Miao women also gave us some pieces of finely embroidered cloth as gifts to take with us. These pieces had fringe similar to the headdresses they wore.

I told the women that we intended to come back, and I invited them to come to the market in Kunming. It would be a good place to sell their wares. Somehow, with gestures and the few words I was able to learn, I conveyed the invitation.

We did stay overnight. When we were ready to leave, I spoke for all of us, "We appreciate what you have taught us, and we have enjoyed your friendship." My words were halting, but I thought they understood.

It wasn't more than a week until Wu returned. He was glad that we were so pleased with our trip.

"How would you like to go to see another area where minorities live? Just you this time--- with me, a pleasure trip for you and a business trip for me; although it will also be a pleasurable jaunt for me having you with me." He touched my shoulder lightly and then rode away.

CHAPTER 17

The first thing I noticed in the Jin Dian, Wu's summer residence, was the beautiful marble used in the building. The idea of visiting the place where it was quarried and seeing the Bai people who lived in the area, was very appealing to me.

"When can we go?" I asked Wu.

"Can you be ready to go early tomorrow morning?"

"Certainly, I could go right now if you want. You have been in Yunnan for a while. I expect that you can point out many things I could never imagine. I'll enjoy traveling. So, what time tomorrow?" I asked.

"At dawn, I'll bring you one of my strongest horses. I know you have your favorite horse, Fleet, but we'll need my powerful war horses to travel. We have to go across small streams, through valleys and up and down forested hillsides. These horses are trained for this. If we're lucky, we may even see some snub-nosed monkeys. Occasionally they come down to the edge of the forests to look for food. You'll find them quite interesting and rather comical looking."

When we had visited the Miao, we could see that most of their homes ranged up a hillside leaving the fertile ground in the valley for intensive rice growing. The Bai people lived in more of a town setting where the stone houses were built next to each other. Cobblestone streets connected them. An old Ming city wall surrounded the town. As we approached Dali, we could see women working in the rice fields. Large, rectangular baskets with rice plants in them were wrapped around their foreheads with ropes. The women were bent over from the load. The scene brought back images of the porters on the Yangtze. I was very much aware of my own easy life. Most people in China worked hard just to stay alive.

We crossed Er Hai, a lake to the east of Dali, on a ferryboat. Immediately, we went to the southern gate of the city. From the top of the gate, the view was extensive. The lake we had just crossed lay shimmering in the sun. Dali was between the lake and a mountain range to the west. We could see three pagodas in the near distance. Our first stop was the market place. It was a riot of color. In addition to the Bai, other minorities were also there to sell their goods. Several people told us that bareback horse riding contests would take place in the morning. I looked at Wu. He saw from my expression that I wanted to watch the races. I hadn't seen any bareback riding since I had done it myself near Shenyang.

Wu said, "The races could be interesting. We'll stay here overnight if that would please you. Now, we can travel to the marble quarry this afternoon. Later, I have some business here."

Delicious fresh fruits were our mid-day meal. My favorite was fried pineapple with coconut. I wanted to learn how to prepare it, so Wu asked the cooks to write the recipe down. None of them could write; consequently, while they dictated it, I wrote it down. Wu liked the pineapple beer best. He said we could find it throughout the region. I was very happy about that. I could drink this beer too without any problems, because it was mild and sweet. After a short ride outside of Dali, we came to the marble quarry.

A workshop stood next to the quarries. Beside it, raw marble columns rose like small mountains. Seeing the veins of different colors was a breathtaking sight. We stood for some time just taking it all in. Then it was time to visit the workshop. The place was animated with men cutting and smoothing the edges of marble pieces. They laid pieces of marble out on benches and on the floor. The pieces ranged from small, thinner slices to large ones that looked far too heavy to move. Two small matching pieces caught my eye. Pale, rose-colored veins in the pieces made them especially attractive. Wu was looking at some of the marble carvings of animals, gods and people. He came over to see what was fascinating me. He felt the edges of one of the pieces for smoothness and hefted it to estimate its weight.

Finally, he turned to me and said, "Would you like to have these? I am sure we could find a good woodworker in Kunming to make table bases for them. Your bronze mirror would look very striking on one of these, and we can find a small marble statue here for the other table. You will have to choose."

I was delighted. I couldn't wish for a better gift. I could feel tears coming into my eyes. Wu had never denied me anything other than what I had wanted most, to be a larger part of his life.

He wiped my eyes. "Here, I thought I would make you happy."

"Oh, you have, you have, but how will we get this marble back to Kunming?"

"I often have shipments of various things going all over the territory by ox cart. It may take a while to get to Kunming, but in the meantime, pick out a carving you like. If it is small enough, we can take it with us. Go pick out something for the second table."

It didn't take me long. I selected a lovely, small carving of Guan Yin. I was very happy, and I still had tomorrow to look forward to.

The morning horse races were more than I had hoped for. I spotted a horse like the Mongolian horse that I rode in Shenyang. The owner and the horse moved as one. The Mongolian was my favorite. Most of the crowd was betting on their favorites in various races. Wu liked a much larger, more aggressive black horse, which was to be in a later race. He took out two silver taels.

"One for you and one for me---at least we won't be betting against each other."

I looked at him with doubt. "A silver tael is too much to bet," I said.

He answered me with an amused smile. "But this way we can win more. We need to place our bets before it's too late."

The men who were in charge of the races looked surprised to see such large bets, but, of course, part of the purse would go to them if we won, so they happily accepted the taels. I didn't realize that I would be so drawn into the excitement of the race; however, I was soon yelling as much as anyone. Wu kept giving me amused glances.

For the race, posts stood at each end of a long field. The horses were to make a full circle of the posts six times. Men stood along the course to count the number of circles the racers made and to insure that there was no foul play among the riders. My Mongolian was slow to start. He remained at the back of the pack during the first circle, but in the second circle, he moved up. With each circle, he gained ground so that by the fifth circle, he and two other horses were neck and neck. As the sixth circle started, one of the three tripped rounding the post and fell. It took an agonizing amount of time for my horse and the other horse left to close in on the finish. Then with a burst of speed, my horse crossed the line. I was thrilled and began jumping up and down with excitement. Wu laughed and said, "My, aren't we lively today!"

He came with me to collect my winnings. I held eight silver taels in my hands. I was rich! I tucked them carefully in my purse while we waited for Wu's horse to race. We looked at some of the stalls where people had set up goods to be sold near the racetrack. The owners were doing a brisk business. At a stall with combs and brushes, I bought four combs made from animal bones, one for Mamu, one for Girten, one for Mei Hua and one for myself.

At another stall, I bought Master Yang and Gaoxing brushes for calligraphy. A fourth stall displayed scrolls and small rice paper books. A small book seemed just the gift for Feng. He had advanced so much in his reading and writing since Master Yang was teaching us. I ventured a guess to Wu that Long Qiong might also like a little book. Wu looked taken aback.

He said, "I don't even know whether he can read or not. I've never bought him a gift."

I was feeling bold, so I replied, "I know you value his loyalty." I added, "He can probably read. Why don't you buy a book for him? If he can't read it, he can give it to Feng."

My insides quivered after I suggested that. Who was I to give Wu suggestions about what he might do? And, what strange impulse made me do that?

Wu didn't seem affronted by my suggestion. He just grumbled and said, "Pick one out, but not one too expensive mind you."

I settled on a book of ghost stories. Even if Long wasn't superstitious, it was neutral enough and should be interesting--- nothing political, philosophical or religious. I was quite certain that he could read.

Soon, it was time for the race. Wu bet his tael on the large black horse. Again, we were both tense. Wu's horse and rider started with a burst of speed, but a smaller brown horse kept up with him. During the whole race, these two switched places. It was only in the final stretch that Wu's horse came alive and dashed across the finish line. Wu picked me up and whirled me around. "Ha," he shouted, "now, we are both rich for the day! Things couldn't be better. This evening we can go in search of cormorants."

I didn't know what to say in response, and I still didn't know who or what the cormorants were. I was not about to ask.

After our evening meal, we both dressed simply with our warm cloaks over our clothes. Advancing toward the lake, Wu cautioned me to be very quiet. As we got closer, I could see several boats with their owners and strange birds on them.

Ah ha, I thought. Cormorants are either the men or the birds, most likely the birds. I had never seen any like them. They looked like a cross between geese and ducks. But what was so special about them? As we got even closer, I saw that these strange creatures had hemp cords around their necks. They stayed within range of the fishermen's lanterns.

Wu whispered, "Now watch."

A bird would dive into the water and come up on the boat with a fish in its mouth, but it wasn't able to swallow its catch because of the cords around its neck. The boatmen quickly grabbed the fish from the cormorants' mouths and somehow made the birds dive back in to catch more fish. Soon many of the boatmen had a large bucket of quivering fish. When the bucket was full, the owners of the boats untied the hemp around the bird's necks and gave each of them one of the fish to eat.

"Very clever fishermen," said Wu. "The birds do all the work."

We both laughed.

The next morning we started back to Kunming by a different route.

"If we go around the top of the lake rather than across it, we might see animals different from any you have ever seen. We can take a little side trip by foot into the lower edge of the mountains. I hope we can spot some snubbed-nosed monkeys."

Our horses were able to do anything, climb through forested mountains or make fast time on the level. They didn't even seem to mind going through shallow rivers or bogs. In the late afternoon, Wu decided that we would stop.

He said, "We'll tie our horses onto this tree right here; then, we'll go up this path at the base of the mountain. If we are very quiet, we may see some monkeys looking for food. They often come to the lower part of the mountain towards evening to forage."

After trekking up the path for about an hour, we came to a fallen log.

Wu said, "This is a good place to sit. If we are very quiet, the monkeys may ignore us. Usually, the monkeys stay high up the mountain, but occasionally they come down to this level for a drink or to look for lower blooming fruit."

My muscles began to cramp after about an hour. I was ready to give up our vigil when Wu tapped me on my knee. To our right, a small group of monkeys scurried down near us. They didn't notice us; instead, they concentrated on lichen in the trees. They made noises, but never opened their mouths to do so. We waited until they scampered back up the mountainside before moving on.

"Did you enjoy seeing them?" Wu said, "I have only seen them once before myself."

I was very happy that he had taken the time so that I could have this experience.

Our horses were waiting for us. We started on to find a place to sleep before night fell. Soon, we found a small inn. The innkeeper gave us separate rooms, but I didn't mind. I was very tired from our adventures.

The next morning, we started for Kunming. We stopped to buy rice cakes and juices for our lunch. As we sat there, Wu said, "I have wanted to tell you what I have decided. Goaxing has proven to be a skillful calligrapher. He is also good at composing letters. I intend to have him travel with my army. He will be very useful to me. He can compose difficult letters for me, put them in his own calligraphy and do small chores."

I was distressed when I heard his idea. Gaoxing was my life. I felt I couldn't do without him near me. I wasn't able to respond for a minute. Then I said, "But..."

Wu didn't let me finish. "I know how precious he is to you, but he is a man now and needs some suitable employment. He won't be in battle. I will take care of him well."

There wasn't anything I could say to change his mind. Wu had decided. Nothing would dissuade him.

The rest of the journey to Kunming was somber. We rarely talked, so I was glad to arrive at my home.

When I dismounted from my horse, I ran to Gaoxing and held him tightly in my arms. He was startled by my sudden burst of affection. I explained what Wu had in mind for him. He looked surprised.

Then he said, "My father is right. I do need to make myself useful. I only hope his expeditions don't take me too far away. I will miss being with you terribly."

I had no say in Gaoxing's new responsibilities. Wu suggested that Gaoxing should also join his conferences with his advisors. If he needed to write letters or do small errands, he would know what was in Wu's mind.

I'm not sure whether Wu was appreciating Gaoxing more now that he was older or was just finding someone that he could use.

CHAPTER 18

When we returned from Dali, I set about trying to find a wood worker who could make bases for my two pieces of marble. I had a feeling that I would be spending more time in my sitting room. Wu said he wanted to meet with his closest advisors at the long table in the room where we ate.

"You can tell your cook that there will be extra people for dinner certain evenings. I'll let you know when we are going to meet. After the meal is over, I will expect everyone in your household to leave the table so that my men and I can make plans."

Ordinarily, I wouldn't have minded, but the thought of Xi Chu eating at my table galled me. But it was my table only because of Wu's generosity. On those evenings, I made a pretext of helping our cook to clean up and take care of any leftover food. In that way, I could eavesdrop on the conversations of Wu and his advisors. I learned what might be happening in the future. Often the army went into different territories in Yunnan to learn how to deal with various military challenges in mountains, swamps or forests.

One evening when Wu was there with his staff, I could hear the beginnings of a heated argument. Rumors had reached Wu concerning the emperor's displeasure over the cost of sustaining the armies of the Three Feudatories. Xi Chu suggested that Wu could strengthen the emperor's approval if his army were to go into Burma to capture the last Ming pretender, and then execute him, his son and all his followers.

Xi Chu said, "I'm sure the emperor will hold you in high esteem if you wipe out the last claimants to the empire."

Long Qiong responded the way I would have. He said, "If you destroy this last remnant of the Ming Dynasty, then the emperor will feel no need to keep a large army in this area. The Ming pretender is no threat while he is in Burma."

Wu replied, "I am a favorite of the emperor. He has relied on the armies of the Three Feudatories to wipe out dissent, and he certainly gains money for the imperial coffers from my feudatory."

The arguments continued. Suddenly, I decided to be daring. I quickly entered the room and said, "I want to be a member of your council."

There was a stunned silence. Xi Chu was the first to respond. "She must be crazy," he said. "She's a woman."

Wu looked at me in disbelief. His face turned red with rage. He shouted, "Woman, what are you thinking? Leave, now!"

My yearning for independence made me a laughing stock. I ran quickly to my room in shame and anger. I hoped Long's points seemed sensible to Wu, but in the morning, I learned that Xi Chu's idea had won out. The Ming pretender had asked for and received sanctuary with the Burmese king. I couldn't imagine what Wu and his army might do to persuade the king of Burma to release the Ming Prince of Kuei, the pretender to the throne, along with his followers, but I also knew how determined Wu could be.

It wasn't long before Wu, his counselors, and a sizable contingent of soldiers were assembled. As always, they looked resolute and brave, but even if the capture was easy, I couldn't imagine the expedition to be ultimately to Wu's advantage. I suppose I must be superstitious, but I felt a heavy cloud pass over our future.

It was strange in Kunming not having the heads of Wu's army and a large number of soldiers there. Gaoxing was able to remain with me, because Wu felt there would be no need for letters on this expedition.

We were all subdued wondering what was happening. On the third day after they left, I saw a small group of men approaching our house. I jumped on my horse and rode out toward the group.

Something was wrong. When I came up to them, I saw Long Qiong with a blood-soaked cloth around his thigh. He was held onto his horse by a soldier riding behind him on the same horse. He slumped over the neck of his mount. He looked as though he was in great pain. Had they already met resistance from the Ming Pretender? One of the men told me what had happened. Wu's forces were near the Burmese border. They met no opposing forces, but Long's horse was panicked by a large snake. The horse reared up throwing Long onto a sharp rock formation. One especially ragged rock had pierced his thigh causing a deep gash. Wu was sending him back with the idea that I could care for him in our house. We got him to the house and into Girten's bedroom because it was on the first floor. Girten could sleep in my sitting room for a while. I felt Long's forehead. It was blazing hot. He must have an infection. I wasn't sure what I should do. I sent Girten to the market to find something to reduce his fever and help with the pain. We also needed to clean the wound well and cover it with a soothing poultice to hasten the healing. Long was delirious; he kept asking where he was.

I took the cloth off his leg only to find the gash red, deep and angrily inflamed. I asked several of the soldiers to hold him down while I lanced the wound. Girten returned with the medicines I needed. I cleaned the wound as well as I could. Then I applied one of the lotions and rewrapped his leg. If things got worse, I didn't know what I would do.

I sat at his bedside for two days and nights. One of the things Girten bought was a sleeping potion. After I gave it to him, he quit tossing around and fell into a profound sleep.

In the afternoon of the second day, Mamu appeared at the door with her hands on her hips. Shaking her head she began to scold me. "Bourtai, if you don't get some rest, you won't be of any help to Long Qiong or anyone else for that matter. Get some sleep. I'll sit with him for a while."

I knew she was right, and I suddenly realized that I was about to fall off my bench.

I replied, "You're right. I won't need much sleep. Please call me if there is any change in his condition."

I went into the kitchen to consult with Yin on what would be best for Long to eat. I thought that juices should be prepared to keep him from getting dehydrated. The cook agreed.

He said, "I know of several mild puddings he could probably eat and perhaps some warm oats."

I was grateful for his suggestions.

"I will let you know how he responds to dishes you make. Try anything you think he might like."

Then I went straight to my bed. I fell into a heavy sleep during which many confusing and disturbing thoughts roamed through my head, but when I awakened, I couldn't remember what they were. I slept into the early morning. Then I woke with a start when I remembered Long's condition. I dressed hastily and went down to relieve Mamu.

When I went into the room Mamu smiled. She said, "He is still sleeping, but I think his fever is gone. At one point he asked for a drink. I ran to the kitchen and got some pineapple juice. He downed it quickly then fell back to sleep. With the first light of the morning, he raised himself up, looked around, and began questioning me. He moved his leg and moaned."

"I know something is very wrong with my leg, but what happened; how serious is it?" he asked.

I replied, "It was quite serious, but I think you are recovering. You will have to stay in bed for some time, but I'm happy about your improvement. You need to have your dressing changed later today. I know it's painful, but we must make sure that the infection doesn't return."

"So then, you are my doctor?"

"Yes, that is what Wu requested. It is also what I want to do. Now, would you like me to read to you?"

"As much as that would be most pleasant, can we just talk for a while? Most of my soldiers are hesitant to talk to me because they think it might be seen as currying my favor. The general isn't much of a talker and Xi Chu and I can never seem to agree on much. I rarely get to talk to a woman and an intelligent woman at that. I'm tired of discussing war strategy. How long have I been here? I wish we knew what is happening with the expedition to Burma. There is much rugged terrain to cross between here and Burma which is said to be a wild land. I'm afraid the end result of this campaign may not be good. I had no stomach for chasing after someone who had so few backers and was so weak that he had to flee China, but I certainly did not want this wound that put me on the sidelines."

"Yes," I said, "I agree with you. And I think going into Burma is sheer folly. But we can't do anything about Wu's ideas. Tell me about yourself. Are you from Shenyang also?"

Long looked pleased by my interest. He said, "Yes I was born there and was in the Manchu army until Dorgon decided that he needed someone reliable to accompany Wu and make sure that he remained loyal."

I asked, "Do you still have family in Shenyang?"

"I do, although my parents both died at the same time of some kind of illness. I have a lovely daughter, Jade. My wife and I were married in an arranged wedding match. It turned out to be a comfortable marriage. My wife's parents had more wealth and a much higher standing in the community than my family had, yet they were happy to have me as a son-in-law. I was gone much of the time on campaigns ordered by Dorgon and Abahai before him; nevertheless, my wife and I were able to have a child after a few years together. We were both excited about the coming birth. I felt fortunate to be close to home for the last few days before my daughter was born. My excitement soon turned to sorrow. My wife died two days after the birth. Even though I greatly mourned the loss of my wife, I loved Jade from the first moment I saw her. Her hair was thick for a baby and she had large dark eyes. I spent hours just watching her and marveling at the miracle she was. I was in a quandary. It was impossible for me to take care of her. I was gone so much of the time. As I was wrestling with my predicament, my wife's mother asked me if she might raise her. She said she felt raising Jade might help her deal with her grief. She promised that she would make sure that Jade would remember me and that I might visit their home whenever I was near enough. I assumed I would be able to see Jade often, but as things have turned out I haven't seen Jade for a number of years. I can write to her now; she is old enough to write back. It's just that I have to imagine what she looks like, what she does, and how her life is going. When I retire, I will go back to Shenyang. By then, though, she may have a family of her own. But enough about me. I have been with Wu San Gui since you were given to him. I know the facts of your life since you were given to Wu, but I know nothing about your thoughts."

My answer startled him. "I wish I were a man. Then I could be independent and do anything I want. I realize I am lucky. Most women have things much harder than I, but being a woman is not a good thing in China."

I didn't want to tax Long; still, I looked forward to our conversations.

Master Yang asked me if I thought Long was well enough to learn chess.

I said, "That is an excellent idea. Chess will take his mind off his wound."

In addition to that diversion, our little musical troop often played our instruments for him in the evening. Long was able to sit up on his bedside to play chess, although he tired very easily. After about a week, he insisted on trying to walk a short distance. He began eating dinner with us at the dinner table. At times, the two of us lingered there. One evening after the others had gone, I looked across the table at Long. Gathering up my courage I said, "Tell me about Chen Yuan Yuan. I understand that Wu rescued her from Li's general."

Long looked a bit disconcerted. He thought for a while. Then he said, "You have probably heard that she is beautiful. Her face is round and full and her eyes are luminous. She is quite aware of her powers. She has only to crook her finger and someone grants her wishes. Her servants seem to be afraid of her. She reminds me of a pampered cat. She has bound feet (golden lotuses) less than five inches long. It must be very difficult to walk, but she uses that impediment to great advantage. When she does walk, she wears long robes of crimson silk that sway slowly as if blown by the wind. Some find this very enchanting. Every thing she does is calculated to show herself in the best light."

I smiled. "You don't sound like she has enchanted you."

He laughed and said, "I suppose I prefer Manchu women who look a little more alive and useful."

"But is she likable?" I asked.

"I would call her vapid, neither kind nor cruel. She is not interested in much other than herself, but I'm sure Wu finds her attractive. It gives him much prestige to be the master of such a renowned beauty." Suddenly, he stared at the floor. He was aware that he had said too much.

Instantly, I found myself voicing my fears. "I know that there are other women, camp followers, women who are a release for passing soldiers. I think about this often, and I am also jealous of Chen Yuan Yuan. Wu and I have a certain intimacy when we are together. It comforts me to remember those times."

I realized that I had revealed too much about my worries.

Long looked at me with a startling intensity. "Intimacy comes in many ways. Just spending time together can bring people closer."

At that moment, I knew why he was always so eager to care for my safety and my needs. I tried not to think about my feelings.

CHAPTER 19

It wasn't long until Wu returned from Burma. He and his men had captured the Ming pretender and his followers. From my house, we heard raucous sounds coming from the camp. Wu and his soldiers brought the Ming pretender and his attendants into Yunnan. Then they transferred their captives to Kunming so that the whole army could witness their deaths. I heard that Wu personally strangled all the members of the group with a silk cord, leaving the pretender for last. This was an excessively cruel act just to make Wu look fierce to his men.

To me, these acts only showed that Wu was becoming less human and more of a monster. When I was younger, I had tried to repress the scenes of his revenge on Ma Xun in my mind. I relived that time when I found out that Gaoxing was blind. Had fate or some god exacted punishment on us because of Wu's cruel revenge?

At times Wu was very generous. Our trip to Dali had been a happy interlude, but I was seeing more and more of the other side of him. It was as though two different men possessed him, one the man I had dreamed of, the other, a savage. I no longer wanted to be with him.

He brought me a beautifully carved jade bracelet from Burma but the result of his expedition tainted the gift for me. I wore it only when I knew he would be around. Wu was a different man from the man I had first imagined him to be. It would not be wise to offend him.

My family, Gaoxing, Mamu, Master Yang, Feng, Girten and Mei Hua had settled into Kunming easily. Feng was delighted to have Mei Hua with us, because, from her birth, she was a favorite of his. As I had predicted to Mamu, Wu had not bothered to do the arithmetic necessary to realize that Mei Hua was the child I had borne when I was first pregnant.

Now, instead of wanting to see more of Wu, I was actually happier when he was gone. He often went away to oversee his monopolies of copper, ginseng, rhubarb, silver and gold in territories as far north as Sichuan and as far east as Guizhou.

Meanwhile the days turned to years and my family and I were happy in Kunming. We grew our own vegetables. We played games with each other. We also learned many of the customs of the peoples of Yunnan as we traveled near Kunming. We spent more time visiting the various minorities. We also learned to fish, and I was able to attend to my painting. Gaoxing often went with his father when Wu needed someone who was especially able to communicate with men who were important to the advancement of his plans. Wu began returning to Kunming only when it was necessary to settle problems and distribute the silver taels that the emperor sent from Peking. These were the allotment for maintaining the soldiers of the southwestern feudatory. His returns always disrupted the smooth functioning of our lives. Wu and I had both changed over the years.

I was told that the leaders of the other two Feudatories had petitioned the emperor asking him to relieve them of their posts. Shang Ko Xi was very old at this point. He wanted to turn his feudatory over to his son. The emperor accepted his petition, but refused to turn the feudatory over to Shang's son. Keng Qing Chung also petitioned to be relieved from his post. He wanted to be transferred with his army back to Liaodong. When Wu learned that the emperor dissolved those two feudatories, he gathered his lieutenants, generals and counselors together to plan his next move. I listened to many of their discussions. He decided that he would attack the aborigines in the northeast of China. I had definite opinions about what he needed to do. Attacking the aborigines would be foolish. They bothered no one, and they stayed in one small area of Yunnan Province. By the end of the consultation, even though most of his counselors disagreed, Wu decided to attack the settlement of aborigines in the far northeastern corner of Yunnan to prove to the emperor that he was still needed in the southwest. Surely, the emperor would be pleased. Long was very emphatic in telling Wu that the aborigines never bothered anyone else in Yunnan, but Xi Chu agreed with Wu. Wu set off with a battalion of his army to make war on the aborigines. He was not aware that the emperor had the same estimate of the aborigines that Long had. In the emperor's eyes, Wu's attacks seemed senseless, a waste of energy and money. Obviously, war with the aborigines did not impress the emperor. Some other strategy would have to be employed. Thus, Wu decided that he, too, should petition the Kangxi Emperor, and ask to be relieved of his post. Wu was certain that the emperor would turn down his petition.

He said, "I have given great service to the Qing Empire. I know the emperor realizes how valuable I am."

Unfortunately, this tactic of petitioning didn't work; instead, the emperor felt he now had no need for a large contingent of soldiers in the southwest. Thus, he agreed to relieve Wu.

When Wu heard about the emperor's decision, he was furious. He had 70,000 men in his army. He could do whatever he wanted. It would be difficult to support such a large number, but Wu was sure that he could use the funds from his monopolies to pay his soldiers. Wu began to curse the emperor and take his rage out on anyone near to him. He drew his advisors together and decided that he was strong enough to challenge the emperor. He established himself as the ruler of a new Zhou kingdom. I heard the conclusion of the meeting.

Later that night, I couldn't sleep. Would Wu's declaration mean war? Wu said he would stay with us for the night; consequently, I was perplexed when he didn't come to my bedroom. My bedroom along with those of Feng, Gaoxing and Master Yang were on the upper floor. The small room at the far end of the gallery was set up for Wu. It overlooked the first floor where the rest of the household slept. I moved quietly to the balcony to try to hear whether the planning session was over. Instead, I heard muffled cries and noises below. I crept to Wu's bedroom. He wasn't there. I moved quietly down several stairs and could see into Mei Hua's bedroom. Wu and Mei Hua lay entwined on her bed. I let out a short gasp and started toward her room. Suddenly, someone grabbed me from behind. A firm hand encircled my mouth. Feng had followed me and held me back. He whispered an urgent caution in my ear.

"My Lady, return to bed! If you interrupt Wu now, there is no telling what he might do."

I came to my senses. Both Feng and I returned quietly to our beds. I stumbled into my room, where I wept in both rage and despair. The next morning I arose early. I took my jade bracelet into the center of the kitchen and flung it on the stone floor. It broke in two with a very satisfying sound. I placed the pieces at the head of the table where Wu sat. That morning, he was to leave for Guizhou. He turned pale momentarily when he saw the bracelet. Then, he gave me an appraising glance and swept it into his pocket. I kept my eyes downcast. Feng could not look him in the eyes either. Mei Hua did not appear for breakfast.

Wu muttered, "A quiet farewell! Where are your tongues?"

No one answered. He pushed back his chair and strode to the door. He turned.

"Bourtai, aren't you coming to see me off?"

I was shaking trying to hold my rage in. I answered sharply, "I prefer to stay here!" I ran to my room and collapsed. I heard Wu's voice outside, loud and angry, giving orders to his men. Finally, they were gone. I fell into a fitful sleep. Later, I pulled myself together and went downstairs. By then, everyone was up. I looked at Mei Hua and said, "You have seriously displeased me. You are to be gone from here by tomorrow morning!"

Feng and Girten were shaken. Mamu was just puzzled. Master Yang had remained in his room. Mei Hua looked stricken. Then she raised her head and looked straight at me.

"I'm sorry but the general is the master of this house. He told me it was his right." She flushed. "Where can I go? I have no one."

I answered with a resolve made stronger by anger and hurt pride. "It is not my problem where you go. I am in charge of this house when the general is gone. I will see that you have money so that you don't immediately starve, but I can no longer have you in my house."

At this point Feng stepped forward. "If she goes, I go!"

I looked at him in disbelief. "But Feng, you pledged to stay with me always." I couldn't believe he would go.

Then Girten also answered, "I too will go!"

I tried to hide my shock. Feng had long been my friend and confidant. He always deferred to me. Girten was like my sister. I loved them both, and I had grown to love Mei Hua also.

I waved my hand in dismissal. "Then go! Whoever wants to go with her, go!"

I was determined to control events, not have them control me. I turned sharply and left the room. *We drive the tiger away only to be embraced by the bear.* Much time alone would be my bear and regret would be my tiger. Mamu, Master Yang and I would rattle around in the house that Wu bought. I told Mei Hua, Girten and Feng to take their horses and three extra to make sure that they had fresh horses when they needed them. I also gave them a large amount of taels and smaller coins. Wu had given me way too many. I had saved over half of them. Also, I sold some of my paintings for a good price.

I felt like my heart was being torn out, but I couldn't see any solution to the problem. I simply couldn't live with Wu making love to my daughter and possibly even his daughter. I tried to tell myself that they would be all right. Feng was handy with a number of things including making bracelets from the designs of the Miao women. Recently, he expanded that talent to devising leather belts from the same designs. All three could read and write, and they had musical talents they could use.

I saw Wu for the last time several months later. He declared himself emperor of the Zhou Dynasty. I knew that he might be gone for several years. Before he left, I asked him to instruct several of the soldiers that he left in Kunming to accompany me to visit the Naxi minority in the far north of Yunnan. He responded to my request with surprisingly angry words.

He said, "I forbid you to go there. It is an unhealthy minority. Women are in charge of the whole clan, and the men don't mind. The children don't even know who their fathers are, because the women feel free to welcome several men into their beds. You are absolutely not going to go there!" It took him a while to recover himself. "Forget that."

Finally, he threw a map down tracing a large circle around Yunnan, Guizhou and parts of Sichuan and Guangxi. "All of this area is under my control. This is *my* kingdom. I will be its emperor and you will be one of its most important concubines."

I said, "I preferred just being the gift that Dorgon gave you. Why has this grandiose scheme taken over your mind?" I sighed in resignation. "What is the need? It is too much territory. Do you actually enjoy its administration?"

He glowered at me. "The administration I can eventually leave to my sons and grandsons, but the conquest...that is my life. My large army keeps order in this whole territory. Once I defeat the emperor, I will reign over all of China!"

I looked at him and said, "I think the Kangxi Emperor is right. You intended to help keep China together at the fall of the Ming Dynasty. Now, your power here has gone to your head. You are a land-hungry madman."

Wu reached across the table and slapped my face. In the past he hurt me cruelly by seeking other women, but he had never hit me in anger.

I put my hand on my stinging cheek. "You are a changed man; I barely know you." I walked to the door trying to hold back tears.

"Go then," he said harshly.

That was the last time I saw him. The Kangxi Emperor summoned Wu to Peking. He intended to reassign him. Wu was infuriated. He contacted many generals in the southern and eastern Feudatories suggesting that they join his rebellion against the emperor. Most of them agreed. The Rebellion of the Three Feudatories began in 1673. Wu was the strongest leader with the most loyal army. The enterprise seemed to go well at first. I worried constantly about Gaoxing. I knew he did not go into battle, but, if Wu's forces were defeated, Gaoxing could be in great danger.

I was able to follow Wu's advances by hearing his reports to the forces he left behind. His army moved swiftly from Yunnan to Henan Province, but then his drive toward Peking bogged down. Many of the generals who had first sided with Wu were suddenly battling the emperor's troops. A number of those generals surrendered to the throne. Wu might have moved his troops northward to Peking and prevailed, but for some reason he settled in Henan. The Khangxi Emperor had cannons that were built under the directions of a Jesuit priest. The cannons were not easy to move; however, ranged to the south of Peking, they made good defense points against further incursions.

Wu began to collect taxes and goods as he advanced. He was in Henan for over two years. This drained the province dry of food and taxes. The peasants were ruined. They could no longer support Wu's army. Before leaving Yunan, Wu demanded that Gaoxing accompany him to write his missives to other members of the rebellion. Gaoxing could compose a very persuasive letter, yet no reliable postal system was available to Wu. At times, the emperor's troops intercepted the couriers. At other times, the appeals for help were too slow. His allies changed their minds and went to the emperor's side.

Gaoxing knew how the rebellion was progressing, so he kept me informed in short letters he sent to me by whatever messenger he could find. I was glad that Long Qiong was there to help Gaoxing. Besides his other duties, Gaoxing was instructed to compose circulars urging people to follow the newly established Zhou Dynasty. Wu's men distributed these to anyone who was within a wide area of the headquarters in Henan.

Our life back in Kunming seemed to plod on, one day, one month, one year after another. I went riding every day to exercise our horses. In this way I, also, got exercise. I felt a great sense of freedom when I was galloping on my horse through the plains, yet the images of Feng, Girten and Mei Hua never gave me a moment's peace. I was constantly worried about their safety, and felt great regret over what I had done. Master Yang made visits to the Buddhist monastery, Yuantong Si, in Kunming. I'm sure he would have joined the monastery if Mamu and I would not have been left alone in our house. The letters I received from Gaoxing grew shorter and were less optimistic.

CHAPTER 20

I had heard about the Naxis from some of the women who gathered in the market place in Kunming. They described a clan in which women were in charge of almost everything. I was very curious to find out more about them. I knew that this clan lived in the far north of Yunnan Province. This is the clan that Wu forbade me to visit. I expected to be alone for some time. For now, I was in charge of my own life. I could do as I wanted. I was competent. I WOULD travel to visit the Naxi. I remembered the route to Dali. I would travel only by day and stay in inns by night. I hoped that I could find someone in Dali who knew the Naxi dialect. I would pay him or her well to accompany me there and work as my interpreter. Of course the person I found to do this would need to understand *putonghua* also.

I was sure someone could be found. I didn't want to take any of the soldiers left in Kunming, because Wu forbade me to take the trip and would probably deal severely with anyone who went with me. I was strong and could surely manage on my own. I also decided that I would take my own horse, Fleet, even though Wu insisted on a war horse for our previous trip to Dali.

That night, I gathered what I would need. I found one of Wu's broad swords and also took my own bow and arrows plus food and a water jug. In the morning, I set off on my trusted Mongolian horse, Fleet. The first part of the trip felt easy, but by the time I arrived in Dali, I was exhausted. I didn't want to sleep until I found the interpreter I needed. The people at the inn were amazed that I was traveling alone; however, they were very helpful and soon found me the kind of interpreter I needed. I was served a more elaborate meal than most travelers received. I think the people at the inn remembered that I had been there with the famous general Wu.

My interpreter, Yufeng, was an old man who apparently knew a number of dialects. I rented a horse for him and we began what turned out to be a more difficult journey than the trip to Dali. After several days, we arrived at one of the small Naxi villages. The village people found a place for Yufeng and his horse where he could stay outside the village proper. I was made to leave my weapons outside with him, but I was welcomed inside. What I had heard was true. This is a matriarchal society. Because the Naxi women choose any man they like to spend the night with them in their hut, it is difficult to tell who has fathered the children. A woman's brother acts as an uncle for any child; even so, the children are loved by all the men and women in the village.

The predominance of the female is even reflected in their language. A female stone is a boulder whereas a male stone is merely a pebble. Their religion incorporates many Daoist, Tibetan and older animistic beliefs. This minority uses pictographs to express themselves in writing.

I was made very welcome. A bed was set up for me in the hut of the main matriarch. That evening, the villagers built a large bonfire and everyone there gathered round it. The singing and dancing were quite lively. They gave me more food than I could possibly eat. In the morning Yufeng was admitted into the circle of huts so that he could translate for me to some of the people. The village was a very happy place. I hated to leave, but I needed to return Yufeng to his home and then head back to mine. I gathered my sword and my bow and arrows. Because of Yufeng's age, we returned more slowly than I would have gone. In Dali, I thanked him profusely and paid him a generous amount. I spent another night at the inn and rose early in the morning to begin my trek back.

As I rode, I thought about my adventure and wondered why every society I had ever known was patriarchal.

I made good time. I traveled far that day and was happy to find an inn for the night. By the next evening, I should be back in Kunming. I enjoyed riding on a path beside a river. I was feeling very carefree and satisfied with the travel I accomplished by myself. The sound of the river was soothing and the air was light, but Fleet began to act nervous. I soon knew why. I heard a rustling in the brush near us. It had to be a rather large animal. Quickly slipping off the horse, I grabbed the broad sword. Turning toward the noise, I saw a wild boar running at me. I faced it head on and drove the sword into its snout. It took a few more steps and then dropped. I realized I was shaking badly and my heart was pounding. Fleet was also shaking. I gave both of us time to stand there to recover.

As we stood there, the wind whipped up and the sky began to darken. Rain began to pelt down. Then suddenly a large crash of thunder frightened Fleet. He began racing down the path. I tried to run and catch him, but I slipped on some gravel and fell. Fleet ran away so rapidly that he was soon out of sight. I tried to stand. My leg buckled. Surely, I hadn't broken my ankle! To my despair, that seemed to be the case. I had nothing to lean on but the broadsword which was rather short and bloody. I limped in the direction of home for a few minutes. Finally, I knew I couldn't go on. I looked for a place to shelter along the path. I hoped there were no more boars around. Night fell. My bid for real independence was a failure. I lay there in the dark berating myself for my hubris and crying like any ordinary woman. Now, I could only hope that someone would find me.

By morning, my ankle was swollen to about twice its size. The pain was gnawing. I lay there several more hours. Eventually, I heard someone coming towards me. It was Yin, my cook, along with several soldiers who would balance me on my horse and return me home where I could have my ankle taken care of. The previous night, Fleet made the trip home and was wandering around outside of the kitchen door. This was what alerted Yin to come looking for me.

I was so ashamed. Here I was, merely a woman who needed to be looked after.

CHAPTER 21

Lately, Mamu was saying that she was extremely tired. Master Yang and I did everything we could to make her feel better, but nothing we did helped her. She was eating much less and sleeping much more. One morning when she did not appear for breakfast, I went into her room to waken her. She seemed to be sleeping, but when I touched her, she felt ice cold. I stayed at her side crying. She had been with me almost all of my life. I could not believe that she was gone. Master Yang began to look for us. When he saw us, he knew immediately what had happened. He also began to cry quietly. We buried her on a lovely hill near Kunming. I told Master Yang that he should now feel free to join the Yuantong Si monastery.

He replied, "There may be time enough for me to do that, but I won't leave this house as long as you are here. You are like a daughter to me."

I began to spend more and more time riding. Often I rode from morning until dusk. It was the only way to ease my mourning. I was out riding one day when I saw a horse and rider coming toward me. It was Long Qiong. Seeing him frightened me. Had something gone wrong? He gave me a letter from Wu. It read:

My Special Horsewoman,

I did not expect to miss you so much, but I must confess that talking with you is like talking to my better self. How can I explain it so that you will understand? I am always the general, always the one who is in command. I can't permit a moment's weakness. Sometimes it is very hard to bear and too much to expect of anyone. I'm constantly planning, never showing doubt or fear. I know I have become a model of what a true soldier must be. I am trapped within this mold. If I am irresolute, I may die. This is hard to contemplate, but the power of who I am is moving me forward in a grand dream. I embrace the feelings of ascendance and cannot give them up. Still, there are times when I want to be ordinary. I want to be alone or only with you. You let me remove my mask and be the other person I might have been. It may be months until I see you again. I think of you often. Know that I am well and my pursuits go forward.

Your General,
Wu

Long watched me while I read the letter. He said, "I'm afraid the general is being too optimistic. Things are not progressing as well as he had hoped." Then Long hesitated. He said "If General Wu's enterprise should go wrong, you will not be safe here. Wu's family in Peking was executed last month. When Chen Yuan Yuan heard that, she left Peking hurriedly for a nearby nunnery. I would suggest that you leave here. Our countrymen always flock to the winner and are cruel to the losers. Emei Shan is not too far from here. We can get there in two or three days. It is a mountain of great beauty, and you would be safe there. I know that, in addition to the many monasteries on Emei, there are also a number of fine nunneries scattered over the mountain. Emei is huge. I can accompany you there."

I asked, "How is it that you are free to do this?"

"Wu sends me and a few others he trusts throughout the country to persuade men to join him. I travel more than I am in camp. I have another letter for you. It is from Gaoxing."

My hands were shaking as I took the letter. It read:

To my most honorable and loving Mother,

This may be the last you will hear from me for a while.

I have spent many sleepless nights trying to determine the course I should take. Ambition has infected my father's mind like a fever. He spins out strands of intrigues into such complex webs that no one knows what he intends. Xi Chu gives him bad advice and feeds his fears. Long Qiong tries to counter that advice, but often fails. All father's generals are afraid to make a wrong move or express their ideas. He has become so suspicious of everyone that he relieves some of his most competent men on hearing the most absurd rumors. Recently he has executed some of his generals.

A while ago, he asked me to compose a letter to a general in the east enlisting him to join the rebel forces. I wrote the most persuasive letter I could, but the general sent back a letter saying that he would not risk joining the rebels. Immediately, when he read the letter, father flew into a rage. He told me to leave. He shouted that I was a disappointment as a son. He said he never wanted to see my face again. His fury frightened me greatly.

Long Qiong has helped me to travel to the home of his cousin west of Henan Province. The family is treating me well, but they are very poor. I will have to find some way to be useful. I may not be able to get messages to you from here, but I will think of you every day, pray for you, and hope to see you some time in the future.

Your obedient, respectful and loving son,
Wu Gaoxing

I needed to think. I looked around my home. Both good and bad had happened here. How could I leave? But leaving a place of memories wasn't always the wrong thing to do. Mamu's grave was near here; nevertheless, I would always have her memory with me anywhere I went. Gaoxing's letter convinced me that I should go. I asked Long to wait until morning. I wanted to store up visual memories of this place. I needed to walk around the area and then sleep on my decision. Long agreed.

By the next morning, I was able to leave. It took me little time to pack---some books, paper, my paints, a few clothes, and my mirror. I wouldn't need much more. Wu had left me an enormous amount of silver taels that the Kangxi Emperor had assigned for his use. Long urged me to take them all, even though they would be very heavy for our travels.

He said, "We can take several extra replacement horses and put the coins in thick saddlebags on the horses. We can also sew a number of coins in our clothes."

I still had my cloak. I had never removed the coins that I sewed in it for my travel to Kunming. Instead, I had just thrown the cloak into a trunk. I would use the cloak now, although it was much too heavy to wear in the southwest. I had suffered through the heat before; I could do it again. We added some inside pockets to Long's cloak so that he could also carry a number of coins with him.

Long said, "You will be sure to receive a warm welcome bringing treasures to sustain yourself and the nunnery."

We both laughed. Even the pious had the need of money.

Our travels were rough even with our best horses. Many small mountains stood between us and Emei Shan. We also needed to cross a number of streams, many of which were swollen and difficult to get around. At one crossing, the only way forward was to use a rope and tackle across the stream. Apparently, this device served many people in the area. A seat was fashioned of burlap. The men slung the large seat over one of the cables and then tied it at the top. The seat could be detached when it reached the other side. There was a corresponding seat to take people from the other side to this side. I pretended to be brave. I took the seat as though it was a thing I often did. On the way over, the seat swayed perilously. I looked down at the raging waters below and could imagine the river sweeping me away. I had to clamp my mouth tightly in order to keep from screaming.

The men hauled my possessions across the same way. A man connected with the system tied our horses together in a line. He then led them across the stream at a shallower place far down stream. He brought them back to where we were on the other side. We waited anxiously for what seemed a long time before he brought them to us. Despite the rain and angry streams, the weather was otherwise not severe. When it was terribly hot, we threw our cloaks across our horses in front of the saddles.

Our affection for each other made the trip quite tolerable. Neither of us dared to speak beyond the idea of affection.

When we were several *li* from Emei Shan, we stopped to take the scene in. The mountain peaks looked blue in the distance. Because of the constant humidity in the area, each peak seemed veiled in a shroud of mist much as I had imagined from the drawings I had seen so long ago. I felt a newness, and I realized how my misery had encased me in the past.

Long said, "I am told that although mists swirl around the mountain, the humidity is not as bothersome there as it is in the valley."

Everything was magical. I was tempted to gallop straight to the bottom of the mountain. We reached the first monastery before nightfall. Bamboos and nanmu trees framed a magnificent front hall. Exotic flowers grew in profusion around and under the trees. The temple had hundreds of rooms for the monks and any guests who might ask for shelter. Our welcome was a sumptuous vegetable-based meal, some of which tasted like meat. A young acolyte helped us, and told us that we were welcome to stay the night at Huizhong Hall. Not only Buddhists, but Daoists and Confucians were welcome to assemble in the Hall. We followed the young monk who served as our guide. With him, we attended the evening prayer in the main hall. I found it difficult to concentrate, because the hall contained so many wonders. From the incredibly high ceiling, a number of red banners hung down, all with writing which I couldn't decipher from below. Between the massive pillars, colorfully quilted and embroidered kneeling pillows were on the floor for the most important monks. Candles flickered and gave off a comforting glow on the yellow and orange robes of the monks. Long Qiong and I knelt and bowed along with them in concert with their movements even though we didn't understand all of the rituals. After the prayers, our young guide took us to the Hall of the Seven Buddhas of the Past. It was an amazing sight. Each Buddha was huge and imposing with eyes seemingly closed to the world. Their carved garments were elaborately inscribed and consisted of a glowing gold finish. For some reason, their hair was painted blue. Our guide told us that the position of the Buddha's hands had different meanings that I would learn if I chose to remain on Emei.

After our short tour, our guide looked embarrassed. He said, "Forgive me. You must be very tired after your journey, but you should talk to our Eminence regarding your intentions."

He led us into a private study where we bowed to a robed monk who seemed as wrinkled as ancient parchment. He was silent as he looked at us. Long Qiong guessed that he expected us to speak first. I was too inhibited to say anything.

Long began. "Your Eminence, may I present Lady Bourtai? My name is Long Qiong. I am one of the humble servants of the great General Wu San Gui."

The monk gave an enigmatic sigh. Then he said, "I have heard of Wu San Gui. He is causing much trouble. But, you, my lady, why is it you wish to live here?"

I answered, "I no longer fit in the outside world. I would choose to stay on Emei Mountain at a nunnery if you will permit it. I can pay for my keep and even donate to this monastery."

He turned penetrating eyes on me. "And why do you wish this?"

I stammered, "The world… I mean the outside world is no longer where I want to be."

"But I expect you still have attachments to that world. Isn't that so?"

I bowed my head. I couldn't deny what he was saying. There was a long silence. I stole a glance at him. He looked much less forbidding now. He waved for me to come closer.

He said, "It takes a long time to detach from the world, but you are welcome to practice that skill here. There is a nunnery up the mountain, Qianfo (Thousand Buddhas Temple), where you may live. It is not far from Hong Chuping Monastery. The monks there hear news of the world from the monks down here at our monastery. We exchange medicines and other necessary things. Some of our monks can't resist gossiping. How things travel so fast is a mystery. You will hear what you want to hear." He looked at our guide. He gave an almost imperceptible smile of dismissal. He turned to our guide and said, "Our guests must be tired. See to their needs."

We backed out with our heads bowed, our hands in an attitude of prayer. The young monk said, "We eat at the sound of the gong before dawn. Come to the hall where you had your evening meal."

He took each of us to a separate room. The next morning came swiftly. After we ate, I was ready for the trek up the mountain into a new world. Long prepared to leave. I detected moistness in his eyes. I knew that my eyes matched his.

I said, "Will I ever see you again? How can I thank you for all the care you have given me over the years?"

I began to cry. Long, himself, looked distressed. "I don't know what the future holds for me. A madness of the brain has rendered the general unpredictable. He suspects everyone of plotting against him. He has executed some of his most capable generals. He paces his tent at night engaged in imaginary arguments with the Kangxi Emperor. His men fear him." Long looked at the ground shaking his head. Then he said, "If it is the will of the gods, you and I will meet again."

CHAPTER 22

The monk who helped us the night before was my guide up the mountain. Several other monks carried my possessions, especially the heavy taels. The mountain had foothold steps carved into it. The carved steps, reinforced by small pieces of timber, made the climb easier. I realized that many feet from ancient times had taken the same path.

We stopped for a while. My guide said, "Very good, now we are halfway up the mountain."

When he said this, I felt like lying down and not moving. I was already exhausted.

I said to the monk, "Let's rest for a while. Tell me about 'Buddha's Glory'. It must be a wondrous sight."

At this the monk laughed. "Yes, it is quite splendid. I have seen it only once, but it will remain in my mind forever."

Many pilgrims passed us on the climb like a line of industrious ants. I often needed to step aside to let them pass. I certainly would need practice in order to climb more quickly. At least, I had sturdy feet to carry me along.

Farther down the mountain I had seen monkeys that were pursuing the pilgrims.

"What is happening with the monkeys?" I said.

The monk grinned and said, "Some of the pilgrims are foolish. They pack themselves delicious snacks. Of course, the monkeys smell the snacks and pursue the pilgrims in order to get a share. They are very aggressive. Some sit on their victims' shoulders and pull at their clothing. Others attack from the rear and hang on to the person's garments. In any case, the pilgrims soon give up their food so that the monkeys will quit harassing them."

"So that is why we didn't pack any food for our trip?"

"Yes, we will stop at a monastery soon and have our lunch there. We monks consider each other as part of a large family," he replied.

We ate well at the monastery. Then we continued our climb. After a full day, we reached our destination. The head nun greeted us at the doorway. The nunnery had an entrance similar to the red columns of the large monastery at the foot of the mountain. I was startled by the nun's shaven head but encouraged by her warm smile. Her robes were crimson. She clasped my hand between her two warm hands.

"I am Lin Ping," she said bowing, "welcome to our nunnery."

Rolling clouds circled the nunnery on every side. It was different from any place I had ever been, yet I felt a sense of 'home'.

After a full day's climb, I was certainly glad to rest, but Lin Ping pulled me along down a long corridor to the room at the very end. The room was small and bare---just a bed, a writing desk, a lantern and a chamber pot. When I settled in with all the things I brought, my watercolors and ink, the taels and robes, I couldn't help but be a little disappointed. The room was so small. Then, one of the nuns opened the window shutters near the bed. Outside was a vast range of mountains and giant pine trees. Gossamer clouds drifted lazily over the mountains. What could be better to wake to each morning? I settled into the routine of the nunnery---prayers, meals, and what work I could do. The next day, I began setting up my watercolors in secluded spots with astonishing views. Some of the nuns wanted to see what I was doing. They would come very quietly and watch as I painted. I never heard what they reported back, but it seems that they developed a fine reputation for me. Lin Ping, the head nun, came to my room one evening. She complimented me on the watercolor scenes I had hanging there. Then she said, "Can you also do calligraphy?"

I responded, "Well, I have learned calligraphy, but I'm not sure if I am good enough to satisfy what someone might want."

She patted my hand and said, "Would you be willing to practice and see how things go? Several of our monasteries and nunneries would be very happy if you could provide them scrolls of calligraphy with sayings of the Buddhist masters or poems of our ancient poets. It would be a wonderful contribution. The scrolls can be a fine surprise."

I started practicing on poems by Li Bai and Du Fu, who were favorites of mine. I wanted to express the soul of the poems in my writing. After practicing for several months, I felt ready to write. I presented Lin Ping with my best efforts. She was delighted.

She said, "From now on, you can be the mountain's calligrapher."

A young nun by the name of Zhang Xu invited me to go with her to collect herbs. She knew a number of fascinating places to visit on Emei. She happily showed me new wonders of the mountain. We usually stayed away from the main trail up the mountain because of all the pilgrims. Sometimes we had to go up a section of the trail to get to a good place to gather berries. As we got closer to the trail, we came upon a group of four monkeys pummeling a tiny monkey. I was indignant about the four attacking the little monkey. He was making pitiful cries. I ran up to the group and chased his four assailants away. This tiny thing just stood shaking. He eyed me with suspicion. Both Zhang Xu and I were carrying drinking water in gourds. We bathed his wounds, but he was still shaking and just seemed rooted to the spot.

I said, "I'm afraid those aggressive monkeys may come back here and try to finish him off. I'm going to make a sling out of my shawl and take him with us."

Zhang Xu said, "Surely you have heard the Chinese saying that if you save another person from death you are responsible for him the rest of your life," she tittered. "You may have found your lifelong companion."

What she said was true. I couldn't take him into the nunnery, but he could lie outside my window in a basket waiting for me to come outside. He did just that. Soon he was my faithful companion. He was afraid to forage for himself; consequently, I began saving a small portion of my meals for him. Zhang Xu was right. I had set myself up for being responsible for him, possibly for life. He was a very polite companion, even though he did sulk when he didn't get a good meal. People began to call me 'the calligrapher and her monkey'.

Zhang Xu arranged for us to visit Buddha's Glory which was at the summit of Sesheng Cliff. I was powerfully affected by this incredible scene. Circles of blue, orange, red and purple hovered over the top of the mountain. These lights invited the viewer to join them. Monks told me stories about worshipers leaping into the lights in order to become one with them. Instead, these people fell through the illusion to a certain death. I felt that pull myself. It was only with great concentration that I was able to stand with my feet firmly planted on the mountain.

Between my two companions, Zhang Xu and my monkey, whom I named Fu Li, life was very pleasant. Together we made expeditions to many more of the unique places on the mountain. And, I was glad that I was useful in one of the most beautiful places in China. Zhang Xu and I visited several noted places. We traveled together to Xinachi (Elephant Bathing Pool). A statue of a large, white elephant with six tusks delighted both of us. The elephant was over 7 meters tall. An impressive Buddha sat on a golden lotus seat on the elephant's back. Lotus shaped bases served to hold the elephant's feet. I smiled as I remembered the sight of Wu on his elephant in Kunming.

To the east of the temple, a sea of sinuous clouds drifted lazily into changing shapes. I thought a lot about my trip to 'Buddha's Glory'. I could see myself in the colors of the clouds. I lost my sense of self in the moment. It is impossible to convey the feeling I had there. Everything seemed to make up one totality, and I was part of it.

I believe that there is some meaning to life. There must be some way we will all not be lost to each other. Earlier in our lives, Wu and I argued about this. He is a Confucian through and through. He has a sense of what is proper and what is moral according to men's estimates, but his belief is in a humanly constructed sense of order, one that often forgets compassion and care. He is not superstitious as most of our countrymen are. He is a paradox. He is unique in his energy and power. Our history books may neglect him or call him traitor or even double traitor; nevertheless, he is a complex man caught in impossible sets of circumstances. I am the one to tell his story and mine.

I meditate now at many secluded spots on Emei. One day after meditating, I returned to my nunnery to find a young soldier waiting for me.

He said, "My Lady, please come with me. Our physician is certain that General Wu is dying. He is asking for you. He says he cannot die until he sees you again."

I thought, "Why should I go?" But I realized I owed much to Wu.

I turned to look at the young messenger. I said, "I'm much older than I was when I last saw Wu. I'm not sure whether I can still ride that far. Do you realize it must be about a five-day's ride?" I saw his drawn face and realized how stupid my question was. Of course, he had just made that journey himself.

He would not acknowledge my hesitancy. Instead, he said, "We can leave at once if you like. The monks at the bottom of the mountain gave us permission to stay at their monastery tonight. On the journey, I will guard your sleep at night so that you can rest. The General believes you will come and is determined to wait. He asked me to give you this."

I stretched out my hand to receive the object that the messenger had pulled from his shirtfront. It was the jade bracelet from Burma. Where it had split in two, someone had repaired it by looping silver wire through the intricate floral openings. Where the pieces met, the silver made it look as though it should have been part of the original piece.

"The General said to tell you that he carries this with him always."

I couldn't refuse him. I told the messenger to rest while I made provisions for the journey. I didn't want to see Wu as he lay dying! I wanted to remember him as he had been, riding his horse over the plains, yet I knew I would regret it if I didn't attempt to grant this request. It took me just one hour to prepare. We reached the monastery at the bottom of the mountain at dusk. After a night's rest, we set off before dawn the next morning. As to the journey, it was everything I expected it to be, a grueling trek over mountains, through forests and then some of the most desolate country I had ever seen. The second morning, we rode for just a short time when we saw the dust from a horse and rider. It was Long Qiong.

I was too late.

Long gave me an account of Wu's death. "Wu heard horses galloping toward us from a distance. He thought you had arrived at last. Painfully he raised himself from his bed; he refused to let any of us help him. He looked transformed. At that moment, one might have thought he could recover. I rushed in to tell him that the horses were an imperial scouting party. Wu's soldiers quickly destroyed all of them, but that meant that Kangxi's main forces would soon be coming. Wu fell back dead. Many of his soldiers took off in a scattered retreat. Wu's grandson retreated and rallied the forces he could. He would not give up the grand dream. He left immediately; I traveled with him. When the emperor's men arrived at Wu's camp, most of Wu's troops had fled. I was later told that the emperor's men dragged Wu's body outside. Then they hacked it into small pieces. The leader of the forces commanded that the soldiers gather his body pieces into small sacks from which Kangxi's riders would scatter those pieces throughout the empire."

Long continued, "From the camp of Wu's grandson, I left to intercept you."

Long anticipated a shocked response from me. Instead, I responded slowly, "Wu loved China. He would have thought this was an ironic joke, to cover so much territory. And I dare say, it might even have pleased him." I turned to Long. "Would you accompany me back to the foot of Emei? I know that you never approved of the idea of setting up a Zhou Empire, so I imagine you will not want to go back to fight for a useless cause. What will you do now?"

He looked thoughtful. "I will try to return to Shenyang to see Jade, my daughter. By now, she may have a family. I just want to see that she is all right. I will have to take a circuitous route to avoid the emperor's men. Will you be content to stay on Emei? I would like to take you with me, but my life will be so uncertain."

"Emei is my home now. The slower pace of life suits me. I do have friends there. I thought of Fu Li. Yes, I even have a small friend on the mountain."

He replied, "Then I will dream of you on Emei. Life can be so strange. I hope I will see you again."

We talked continuously on the way back to Emei. We stopped at an inn the first night. A full moon rose that night. We sat together talking until shortly before dawn just savoring the fact that we were there and our lives were continuing, maybe in strange ways.

I did mourn Wu's death. When I got back to the mountain, I felt depressed; I avoided the others for a while, but I couldn't ignore Fu Li. Zhang Xu took care of him while I was gone; nevertheless, he jumped up and down when he saw me. This pleased me and lightened my spirits. I returned to my places of meditation, not necessarily to paint, but to gather my strength to be more a part of life now that Wu was gone.

People don't speak openly of him, but they whisper his name and talk about his death with a little shiver of fear. They fear his memory and his ending. Fearing greatness, even misplaced greatness, they try to find some meaning in Wu's life, if only as a cautionary tale. They argue about the symbolism of the emperor's punishment of Wu, but Wu was not superstitious. He would not care to chase after body parts as eunuchs wanted to do. He had faith that I would keep him together in my heart, that here behind my ribs, I would keep him whole.

EPILOGUE

The Kangxi Emperor was not satisfied with Wu's death. He also had all of Wu's family killed. Even Wu's grandsons were eventually captured and executed. Wu had kept on fighting as though his family was still alive. He thought his grandsons would succeed him. Wu would have laughed at Kangxi's efforts to humiliate him, even after death. He had never believed in an afterlife. The belief that a body must be intact to attain a new realm seemed totally ridiculous to him.

I'm not sure what I believe, but the idea that I will never see Wu again is unbearable despite our differences. I returned to my nunnery where I was surrounded by the compassion and concern of the nuns. They watched over me making sure that I ate. But basically I existed in a coma-like sleep. Eventually, after several months, I began to realize that the world still existed and that I was still a part of it.

I was able to respond to Lin Ping's suggestion that I help her gather medicinal herbs for the nunneries and some of the monasteries. Being out on the mountainside among the beautiful forests and streams made me look at the world again and realize how extraordinary life is. I did have a future in it.

Together Lin Ping and I made expeditions to many of the unique areas of Emei Mountain. Once again, I traveled to the summit to view 'Buddha's Glory'. Again, in the wonders of the glowing lights that surrounded the peak of the mountain, I lost my sense of self in the experience. The aura reflected my image so that it seemed that I was just lying in the shimmering colors.

Again, we traveled together to Xiangchi (Elephant bathing pool). To the east of the temple complex, distant mountains seemed to float in and out of a sea of clouds.

I began again to seek out isolated places where I could meditate. One morning as I sat on a high rock with a view of other parts of the mountains and its paths, I saw a man below being led slowly up the path by a young woman. The man was holding a small child. When the threesome came closer, I felt a joy I couldn't immediately identify. As they came further up the mountain, I realized that the man was my son, Wu Gaoxing.

I stumbled toward them shouting, "Gaoxing, Gaoxing." I heard the return cry.

"Mama, Mama."

We came together on the path, embracing, crying and laughing.

"Mama, this is my wife, Zhen Shou." Then holding the child out in front of him, Gaoxing said with pride, "And this is our son, Zhen Liang. To protect him, we don't call him by his surname, but he is a Wu."

In his anger, the Kangxi Emperor thought he had exterminated the family of Wu San Gui. Yet here were two descendants of Wu and two connections to the future!